The Double Horror of Fenley Place

"What's going on?" Nancy asked herself, carefully touching the small lump on her head.

Suddenly the footsteps started again. Nancy held her breath. It was the same sound she had heard earlier that afternoon. Rubber track shoes on roof shingles.

He was on the roof!

Now Nancy knew she had to get out of the attic, and fast. If she didn't, she'd soon be trapped inside while Fenley Place burned around her!

Nancy Drew
Mystery Stories

Available from MINSTREL BOOKS

NANCY DREW®

THE DOUBLE HORROR OF FENLEY PLACE

CAROLYN KEENE

A MINSTREL™ BOOK

PUBLISHED BY POCKET BOOKS

A MINSTREL PAPERBACK *ORIGINAL*

A Minstrel Book published by
POCKET BOOKS, a division of Simon & Schuster, Inc.,
1230 Avenue of the Americas, New York, N.Y. 10020

Cover artwork by Bob Berran
Produced by Mega-Books of New York, Inc.

ISBN: 0-671-64387-8

First Minstrel Books Printing September, 1987

10 9 8 7 6 5 4 3 2 1

NANCY DREW MYSTERY STORIES is a registered trademark
of Simon & Schuster, Inc.

A MINSTREL BOOK and colophon are trademarks
of Simon & Schuster, Inc.

Printed in the U.S.A.

Contents

1

Bess Screams for an Audition

"Aaaaaaaaaarrrrrrhhh!"

A terrifying scream spread through Nancy Drew's house. It was a scream filled with horror and panic and bone-chilling fear.

The moment Nancy Drew heard it, she sprang to her feet. An instant before, she had been reading a magazine on the bed in her sunlit bedroom. But now she was running downstairs in the direction of the hideous sound.

The scream continued. It was coming from the living room, and it seemed to say, "No matter how quickly you reach me, it will be too late."

With her reddish blond hair flying behind her, Nancy reached the bottom of the stairs just as the scream died. Her breath came fast and her blue eyes widened at what she saw.

In the middle of the living room stood Nancy's good friend Bess Marvin. Bess's usually pale skin was flushed from screaming, and there was a look of total terror on her face.

Nancy glanced around the room. What had made

Bess scream? There were no dead bodies on the floor, no bats circling the ceiling like a precision aerial flying team, and no mice. There was only Hannah Gruen sitting on the sofa. The Drews' housekeeper had her fingers in her ears and an expression of intense pain on her face.

"Bess, what is it? What's wrong?"

"Pretty convincing scream, huh?" Bess said. Her voice was calm, and she was smiling.

"It worked for me," Hannah said. "Now I think I'll get back to the kitchen."

When Hannah was gone, Nancy repeated, "Convincing? Bess, you scared me to death!"

"Yes, I know," Bess said, beaming. "And that was just a *rehearsal!*"

"For what?" Nancy asked. "Being eaten alive?"

Bess dramatically brushed her straw blond hair out of her face and produced a yellow sheet of paper from her tote bag.

"Who would believe that a little slip of paper could totally change your life," she said.

"Not another parking ticket," Nancy teased. But she took the paper from Bess and read it.

The photocopied flyer read:

AUDITION!!

WANTED—young female extras who can scream for small parts in new Hank Steinberg horror film. 2:00 P.M. today—at the McCauley house on Highland Avenue!!

* * *

"These signs are all over town," Bess said when Nancy looked up. Her blue eyes sparkled with excitement.

Everyone in River Heights knew that a movie was being filmed in their city. The world-famous movie director Hank Steinberg had chosen Nancy's hometown for the location of his newest film. It was going to be called *Terror Weekend,* and it would undoubtedly be another spine-tingling, stomach-twisting horror masterpiece. And now River Heights citizens were being invited to audition.

For a moment, Nancy thought about being in the movie herself. The lights, the cameras, the action . . . the screams, the murder, the blood. It would be a lot of fun. But then she looked at Bess and knew that Bess wanted a part in Hank Steinberg's movie a lot more than she did. It was one of Nancy Drew's main rules never to compete with her friends for anything important.

"Can you come with me to the audition?" Bess asked. "It's almost two o'clock now."

"Definitely," Nancy said.

"Are you sure?" Bess asked. "I mean, you've been promising to go watch them film for two days, now. Are you positive you don't have some errands to run for your father, or an important case to solve?"

Bess was referring to the fact that Nancy Drew was River Heights' famous young detective. She was known for her ability to solve all kinds of intricate mysteries. She also occasionally helped out her father, Carson Drew, who was a respected attorney.

But Nancy shook her head no to both questions.

"All right. Then let's get out of here before Hannah comes in and asks you to do twelve loads of wash or something," Bess said.

"I heard that," called the voice of Hannah Gruen from the kitchen. Hannah had lived with the family ever since Nancy was three years old.

Bess and Nancy poked their heads into the kitchen and were relieved to find Hannah smiling.

"Go on," Hannah said. "I'll see you later. You can tell me all about these Hollywood horror people then. At dinner?"

"I don't think so," Nancy confessed. "Bess and I will probably eat out."

"All right. I guess I can wait until morning," Hannah said as Nancy and Bess headed for the door.

Once the two girls were in Nancy's blue sports-car, Bess put on a large pair of dark round sunglasses.

"Yesterday I was just someone standing in the crowd," she explained. "But today I have to make an *entrance.*"

The warm summer breeze felt good to Nancy and Bess as they drove down the back roads that led through some of the prettiest residential areas of town. Soon the two girls arrived at Highland Avenue.

Highland Avenue was one of the oldest streets in River Heights. The houses were all large, stately Victorians built almost a hundred years ago. Some of them looked their age—tired, overgrown, and in need of a paint job. Others had been spruced up by young families who had recently moved in. Down the middle of the street stretched a strip of dark green grass, bordered by gravel, with tall trees that shaded most of the roadway.

The street had been blocked off at one end so that Hank Steinberg could park his movie trucks and camper vans. That was the end Nancy had driven to. She parked on Margery Lane, a block away.

"Okay, Bess, let's see that entrance you've been talking about," Nancy said.

Bess stepped slowly out of Nancy's car as if she were being photographed.

It *was* a dramatic entrance—everything Bess had hoped for. Unfortunately, no one but Nancy was there to see her.

The girls walked eagerly down Margery Lane and turned the corner.

"Oh—there's Fenley Place!" Nancy said. "I'd forgotten how spooky that house looks."

On one side of Highland Avenue sat the McCauley house, where *Terror Weekend* was being filmed. Directly across the street from it was Fenley Place—the gloomiest, most sinister-looking house on the street. Garver Fenley, the man who built the house, had died the first night after he moved in. Ever since then, strange stories had been told about the place.

"Don't look," Bess said. "Every time I come over here, I turn my back on that horrible old mansion as quickly as I can."

11

"I know what you mean." Nancy nodded. "Even *I* used to believe that if you passed in front of Fenley Place on the night of a full moon, you'd turn into a werewolf. But that was when I was six."

"You mean it's not true?" Bess said half-seriously.

Nancy laughed. "You're too easy to scare. I remember the Halloween when I was in fifth grade and a bunch of us came to Highland Avenue to trick or treat."

"I remember coming here, too," Bess said, shuddering. "When we passed Fenley Place, I was *positive* I saw a glowing green shape in one of the windows. You could have heard me screaming all the way down the block."

Nancy smiled. "It was your imagination. Anyway, it's just a house. Let's just forget about Fenley Place and go to your audition."

"I'll never forget about it." Bess shuddered again. She purposely walked the long way around the barricades, to stay as far away from Fenley Place as possible.

As they approached the movie location, Bess's thoughts returned to the movie.

"I haven't been able to get near the action," she said. "They've got a hundred security people keeping the crowds away from the McCauley house. But just watch me today."

The hundred security people turned out to be four young men and two young women, all wearing walkie-talkies in their back pockets. But even though they were young, they did their jobs well, with a lot of authority. As a result, the spectators were kept a good distance from all the lights, electrical cables, cameras, and action that filled Highland Avenue.

Bess pushed her way to the front of the crowd and started to cross one of the barricades.

"You again?" a female security guard said to Bess. "I've told you a million times you have to stay back."

Normally, Bess wasn't pushy at all. In fact, it usually took a lot of Nancy's energy just to get her friend involved in one of Nancy's mysterious adventures. But now Bess was really excited. She was determined to get a part in this movie.

Bess said only one word to the security guard, but she said it slowly and dramatically. "Audition."

The young woman rolled her eyes and waved Bess and Nancy by. The girls wandered around among the technicians for a while, trying to figure out where to go.

Noticing their confusion, one of the technicians asked, "Looking for someone?"

"Auditions," Bess repeated, more quickly this time.

"Are you a screamer, a bleeder, or a corpse?" the technician asked without much concern.

"Screamer!" Bess said.

"Brandon," was all the man said, jerking his thumb toward the wide, green lawn of the Mc-Cauley house.

Bess and Nancy walked in the direction the thumb had indicated. But the front yard of the

McCauley house was an obstacle course. There were thick electric cables, fake plastic shrubbery, and large pieces of lighting all over the place.

Finally, they came to a young man wearing a name tag that said Brandon Morris—Casting on it. He was about twenty-five years old, and he wore khaki shorts with a Hawaiian shirt. He was talking to two teenage girls and writing what they said on a clipboard.

"I'm a natural for this," one of the girls said to Brandon. "I have seven sisters. Believe me, I have to yell just to be heard."

Brandon smiled, handed them each a number, and told them to get in line over by the fence. Then he turned to Nancy and Bess.

"Name?" he said to Nancy. "Age?"

"Nancy Drew, eighteen, but I'm just here to watch," she replied.

"Watch quietly," Brandon warned her. "We're setting up a scene right now in the house."

Nancy stepped back while Bess gave Brandon her name, address, age, and telephone number. Just then a prop man came by carrying a stack of books.

"'Scuse me, coming through," he grunted. Nancy had nowhere to go to get out of his way except up the steps of the McCauley house and onto the porch. From there, she realized she could see right into the McCauleys' living room, where the scene was going to be shot.

It only took Nancy an instant to recognize the actor who was starring in the film. Deck Burroughs's dark wavy hair was unmistakable, even

14

from the back. In the scene they were preparing, Deck was standing perfectly still, gazing out a side window. Meanwhile, books were flying off the book shelves and zipping across the room toward Deck's head. Nancy could see that the books actually traveled on very thin, clear plastic wires.

"Hey, Nancy Drew—off the porch!"

It was Brandon's voice behind her. She turned around. Brandon was smiling, but his tone meant business. Then he pointed to Bess, who was waiting her turn to scream. Nancy walked down the porch steps to her friend.

"Good luck, Bess. Don't be nervous," Nancy said, giving Bess's arm a squeeze.

The squeeze took Bess by surprise and she let out a small screech. The other girls in line immediately started complaining.

"Save it for the audition, showoff," grumbled a blond teen standing in front of Bess.

"Yeah, wait your turn," said her friend.

"Do you believe I have to take this from *them?*" Bess said under her breath to Nancy. "They're not even from River Heights!"

Nancy just laughed. "Then they probably don't know how creepy Fenley Place is," she said. "So they won't scream as well as you will."

"Don't remind me," Bess said, turning her back to the house again.

"Relax," Nancy said. "You'll be okay. I'm going to sit on the grass in the center of the street and watch from there." As she left, she held up her crossed fingers to wish Bess luck.

While she waited for the auditions to start, Nancy gazed at the McCauley house in front of her. Normally the three-story, clean white house had a friendly look to it. Its big, wide porch was welcoming, and the apple tree in front usually had a swing hanging from its thickest limb.

But today the swing was gone. Rows of big movie lights attached to tall scaffolding flanked the house. The scaffolding looked like a dinosaur skeleton with gigantic eyes, and it gave the house an unreal, spooky feeling. Broken shutters and cracked windows had also been installed. As a final touch the outside walls had been covered over to look as if they hadn't been painted in years.

Suddenly Nancy heard some gravel crunch behind her. She turned around and saw a pair of running shoes standing next to her. "Screamer, bleeder, or corpse?" asked the voice belonging to the shoes.

Nancy looked up and saw a man in his mid-thirties wearing jeans and a sloppy knit shirt. He carried a walkie-talkie in his back hip pocket, just like the other crew members. But Nancy recognized the face immediately. It was the director, Hank Steinberg.

Nancy got to her feet. "Spectator," she said. "My friend's a screamer."

"Okay," Hank Steinberg said gently and smiled. Then he walked toward the McCauley front lawn.

A moment later the auditions were underway. Brandon called out the numbers and Hank Steinberg listened as various residents of River Heights screamed for their lives.

But between screamer number four and screamer number five, Nancy glanced over at Bess and stiffened. What was it that Bess was staring at and frowning at across the street?

Suddenly Bess's pale skin grew even paler. She pointed across the street at something up in the sky and out of her mouth came an even more terrified scream than Nancy had heard at home, earlier. Then she slumped to the ground in a dead faint.

Hank Steinberg, Brandon, all the screamers, and all the crew looked at Bess—and applauded.

But Nancy knew that there was real horror in Bess's scream. She turned her head in the direction Bess had been pointing, to the roof of Fenley Place.

A cloud of thick red smoke—the color of blood —was billowing out of the chimney as from an open wound.

2

Bloodred Smoke

The eerie crimson cloud puffing out from the
chimney of Fenley Place held Nancy's eyes captive
for just a moment. Then her attention snapped back
to the scene on the McCauley lawn.

Bess lay on the ground, motionless. Brandon
stood over her, his hands on his hips. "Very realis-
tic," he said in mocking voice. "You can get up
now."

"No fair!" the other screamers shouted angrily.
"It wasn't her turn!"

"Let me through," Nancy insisted, pushing her
way through the crowd. "She *really* fainted."
Nancy finally reached the lawn and knelt by her
friend.

It was only a short while before Bess began
to stir. Then she sat straight up like a corpse
in a horror film and began talking in a foggy
voice.

"Did you see it, Nancy? It was coming out of
Fenley Place. I knew I shouldn't have come near
that house. It was the color of *blood.* Did you see
it?"

"What is she talking about?" Brandon asked.

"Red smoke," Bess whispered. "Coming out of the chimney."

Everyone looked at the somber house across the street but the smoke was gone.

"I saw it, Bess," Nancy said seriously. She didn't care that the crew members on hand and the other screamers looked at her as if she and Bess were *both* crazy.

"That's only half of it," Bess said. "Look at my script. This page says a girl walks down the street and suddenly sees *bloodred smoke* coming out of a chimney." She stared at Nancy, her eyes wide. "Isn't that weird?"

Nancy nodded her head slowly in agreement. Just then, Hank Steinberg appeared and stooped down by Bess.

"Are you okay?" he asked.

"I guess so," Bess said. Then, forgetting it was a great opportunity to make an impression on the director, she simply stared back at him.

Hank Steinberg said "Good," then stood up and went back to work with his crew.

When he was gone, Brandon tried to regain everyone's attention. "Okay, girls," he said, "let's get on with the auditions. Mr. Steinberg is very busy." He grinned down at Bess. "Your audition is over."

Bess got to her feet, helped by Nancy. She glanced at her friend. Nancy had a look on her face that Bess recognized immediately. The look said, "There's a logical explanation for this, and

I'm going to find it." She grabbed Bess's arm and they both started walking down the lawn to the street.

"Where are we going?" Bess asked. "And don't say to Fenley Place," she added firmly.

"We have to go across the street and check out the house," Nancy said matter-of-factly.

"Forget it," Bess said. "You can go without me if you want, but I'm not moving an inch." Bess stopped walking and stood in the middle of the street.

"Come on, Bess," Nancy said. "It's just a big ugly house, that's all."

"No, it's *not*," Bess said.

Bess looked across the street at Fenley Place and thought about the stories she had heard all her life. Who knew whether they were all true?

No one who moved into Fenley Place stayed very long. People said the sidewalk in front of the house was always cracked, no matter how many times it was fixed. Bess could *see* that was true. It was rumored that the rusty wrought-iron fence surrounding the house and yard occasionally dripped blood. It was also said that the house itself could tell what kind of a person you were as soon as you walked through the front door. Bess often wondered what horrible things would happen if the house didn't like you.

Nancy kept on walking, and before Bess knew it, her friend had opened the gate, marched up the stone path, and was standing on the shadowy porch of Fenley Place.

"Don't go in there!" Bess yelled. She ran to catch up with her friend. She couldn't let Nancy face that horrible house alone, no matter how scary it was to go with her.

As Bess hurried through the open gate, a sharp point on the wrought-iron fence caught her sleeve and tore it.

"You see?" Bess said. "This house hates me already."

Nancy rang the doorbell once, twice, and again.

"No answer," Nancy said.

"No one home," Bess said, quickly hurrying back down the porch steps.

"The two are not always the same," Nancy pointed out in her logical detective voice. She walked around to the back of the house, and Bess reluctantly followed.

Nancy knocked on the back door, peeked in the side windows, and checked out the garage. It was empty.

"No one home," Nancy concluded. "So where did the smoke come from? It doesn't make sense."

"Hey, you two!" a crusty voice called out. "What do you girls want?"

Nancy and Bess turned around and saw a man in his seventies standing in the driveway, glaring at them. He wore a white shirt with a tie and a cardigan sweater even though it was a hot summer day.

"My name is Nancy Drew, and this is Bess Marvin," Nancy said. The man didn't say anything.

"Do you live here?" Nancy asked politely.

"I'm the next-door neighbor," said the man. "And you two don't look like you're selling Girl Scout cookies, so what are you doing snooping around?"

"Would you tell us who lives in Fenley Place?" Nancy asked.

"Mr. and Mrs. Teppington and their two children," the neighbor answered. "What concern is that to you?"

"Is that the Mrs. Teppington who teaches English at the high school?" Bess asked.

"Yes," the man said grumpily. "Now, look here. We're both asking a lot of questions but *I'm* the only one doing any of the answering."

"Have they gone away?" Nancy asked with a smile.

The man threw his hands up in frustration. "Been gone a week. Coming back soon," he said testily.

"Have you seen anything strange going on here today?" asked Nancy.

"You mean *besides* this conversation and your snooping around?"

Nancy and Bess nodded their heads.

"Young ladies, I've lived next door to this place for forty years. I've seen enough strange things to fill a dozen scrapbooks."

"Have you ever seen red smoke come out of the chimney?" Bess asked.

The man squinted one eye at her. "No. Have you?"

Bess dropped her voice to a mysterious and dramatic whisper. "Yes," she said.

"Well, I'd suggest you wear a hat and keep out of the sun," the man said. "It'll cut down on the hallucinations."

"We'll come back when the Teppingtons are home," Nancy said to the next-door neighbor. "Thanks. You've been a big help."

The man went back toward his own house, and Bess sped up her exit toward the street.

As Nancy followed along, she began thinking out loud.

"There's no ladder around," she said. "So no one climbed to the roof to set off a flare or anything like that. Someone inside the house had to start the red smoke."

"But there's no one home," Bess said. "Would you please walk a little faster and keep up with me, Nancy? Aaaahh!" Bess screamed.

Bess had walked right into a young man standing at the front corner of the driveway.

"I've been looking for you," he said to Bess.

Nancy recognized him immediately. He was one of the four people working crowd control on the set.

A lock of blond hair hung down into his eyes, and he grinned at both girls with a shy, friendly smile. Like all the crew members, he was wearing a white T-shirt. It said *Terror Weekend* in red letters that looked like blood smears. He had a walkie-talkie hooked to the belt of his white jeans.

"Hello, screamer," he said. "Listen, I'm sorry about what happened before. We didn't realize you fainted for real. Are you okay?"

"How would you feel if you saw bloodred smoke come out of a chimney?" Bess asked.

"I've worked on three Hank Steinberg films," he said. "I guess I'm sort of used to that kind of stuff."

"Well, I'm *not* used to it," Bess said.

"I've got to get back to work in a minute," the young man said. "But Hank sent me to find you. He loved your scream, and he wants you to be in the film."

Bess's face quickly went through about eight different expressions. They registered every emotion from fear of Fenley Place to dreams of major stardom.

"He does?" she finally gasped.

"I wouldn't kid you," the young man said. "Now, what's your name?"

"Fantastic!" Bess said, squeezing Nancy's hands tightly.

"Very unusual name," he said with a laugh.

"Her name is Bess Marvin," Nancy said. "I'm Nancy Drew."

"Hi," the young man said, smiling shyly again. "I'm Chris Hitchcock."

"Hitchcock?" Nancy knew that Alfred Hitchcock had been one of the greatest horror film directors of all time. "Terrific name for someone in the movies."

"Well, it's not my real last name," Chris admitted. "Can you believe *Chris Smith*—instant boring, right? So I changed it. Named myself for one of my idols."

"I like his movies, too," Nancy agreed. "Did you ever see *North by Northwest?*"

"Are you kidding? Of course. Twenty-two times," Chris said. "And I've seen *Psycho* at least ten times."

Bess cleared her throat to get back in the conversation. "So what do you do on this film?" she asked.

"All kinds of stuff. Production assistant, crowd control, and I did the location scouting."

"What's that?" Bess asked.

"Hank said he wanted to film somewhere in this area, so I found River Heights for him. And I picked the McCauley house, too."

"Too bad you're not using Fenley Place," Nancy said. "It's a natural for a horror movie."

"I tried, believe me," Chris said. "And, you know, we pay a lot of money to use someone's house. But Mr. Teppington refused. He didn't care about the money or fame or anything—case closed! He was really nasty about it, too."

"Never say case closed around Nancy Drew," Bess said.

Nancy could tell by the way Chris scrunched his eyebrows that he wanted to know what Bess meant. But he didn't ask.

Instead he said, "I've really got to get back now. Bess, report to Brandon Morris tomorrow morning at eight and he'll take you to wardrobe."

"Do I get one of those T-shirts?" Bess wanted to know.

"Well, actually they're only supposed to go to regular cast and crew members, but . . . I'll see if I can get you one," Chris said. "Hey—maybe you guys can show me around River Heights sometime."

"Sure," Bess called as Chris left them.

She let him get a safe distance away before she burst.

"I'm going to be in a movie! I could just scream!" Bess said. "I knew it would happen the minute I saw those signs. Isn't this great, Nancy?"

It was then that Bess realized Nancy wasn't listening to her. She was staring up at a third-floor window under the roof of Fenley Place with a look of shock and amazement on her face.

The look was enough to turn Bess's blood icy cold.

"Do me a favor," Bess said to Nancy. "If you've just seen something awful, please keep it to yourself and don't tell me. Okay?"

Nancy grabbed Bess's cold, trembling hand and held it tightly.

"I'm just wondering," Nancy began. Her own hand was trembling a bit, too. "If no one's home, why did I just see a woman in a white nightgown standing in the third-floor window?"

3

The Schoolyard Restaurant

"Woman? Nightgown? Window?" Bess said each word slowly and quietly. She still hadn't turned around to look.

"Someone is in there, Bess," Nancy said firmly. "And I want to find out who it is."

Nancy let go of Bess's hand. A moment later Bess realized she was standing all by herself on the front lawn. She turned and shuddered. Fenley Place was looking scarier than ever. But as Bess's eyes scanned the third-floor windows looking for a face, she found nothing.

"Nancy!"

"Pssst!" Nancy answered, giving Bess a wave from the front porch. "Come on up."

Bess didn't budge. Nancy rang the bell more insistently this time, *and* she knocked on the door loudly. While she waited, her foot tapped an impatient rhythm on the porch.

"I don't see anyone in any of the windows up there, Nancy," Bess called. "That old man next door must be right. The Teppingtons *are* gone."

27

Nancy stepped off the porch, looking confused. She glanced up once more at a window under the roof. No one was there.

"Maybe you just *thought* you saw someone," Bess said. "It could have been a reflection from the movie lights across the street. It *is* getting dark, you know."

"Maybe," Nancy said half-heartedly. She didn't have a better explanation herself.

"Let's go," Bess said nervously. "I've got to stay away from this place so I can rest my voice. In fact, I feel a scream coming on *right now!*"

"Okay," Nancy sighed. "I'll drive you home."

"What about dinner?" Bess asked.

"I thought you wanted to rest."

"I said rest. I didn't say *starve!*" Bess said.

Soon the two friends were safely back in Nancy's sportscar, headed toward one of their favorite restaurants—The Schoolyard.

The Schoolyard was one of the most unusual restaurants in River Heights. It was owned by a former cafeteria cook from the high school.

The menu consisted of all school-type foods: sloppy joes, mystery meat, pizza by the slice, burgers, and jello with whipped cream, all served cafeteria style. But unlike the food in most of River Heights' schools, the food at The Schoolyard was delicious.

Bess, Nancy, and their friends loved it. They had spent so much time in school cafeterias that the Schoolyard food had a familiar look, taste, and aroma. And the food came in large quantities for small prices.

"I don't see George yet," Bess said, slipping into a booth in the restaurant.

"She's probably stuck in traffic trying to get around the movie crew."

Nancy and Bess had made plans to meet George Fayne, who was Nancy's other best girlfriend and Bess's cousin.

Although they were cousins, the two girls couldn't have been more unalike.

Bess was short, blond, and a little lazy, while George was tall, thin, dark-haired, and full of energy.

Bess liked to steer clear of danger and action. George liked to think on her feet, and she was always quick to offer an opinion, too.

And unlike Bess, George didn't care about fancy clothes. Bess dressed to be noticed. George dressed to be comfortable—although she had her own style that was flattering to her.

Despite their differences, the two cousins loved each other and always stuck together. And, through thick and thin, they stuck by their best friend, Nancy Drew.

George arrived at The Schoolyard wearing black pants with suspenders and a bright blue T-shirt.

But just as Bess was about to blurt out her exciting news, George started talking. "Hi, Bess. Hi, Nancy. Sorry I'm late, but you won't believe what happened to me, or what I have to tell you!"

She pulled up a chair and sat down with one of her legs folded under the other. "Who wants to hear what Hank Steinberg eats for lunch? Wouldn't you just *die* to know who Deck Burroughs—hunky star of *Terror Weekend*—was talking to at breakfast? And is it true that Jenny Logan, Hank Steinberg's favorite actress, really brings a teddy bear with her to makeup every morning? Guess who knows the answers to these and many more questions? Me!"

"How do you know all this stuff?" Bess asked, leaning toward her cousin expectantly.

Nancy was silent, watching a splash of milk form a thick cloud in her iced tea. Her faraway look did not escape George's attention.

"I got a new part-time job today," George explained. "I'm a food server for Elegant Eats. You know, it's Pat Ellis's catering service, which is feeding the movie people while they're in town. I will be handing Deck Burroughs his breakfast, lunch, and dinner just about every day until he leaves River Heights. Do you believe it?"

"Well, maybe you'll be handing me my meal, too," Bess said to her cousin. "Because today Hank Steinberg chose *me* to be in his movie."

George's mouth flew open. "A part in the movie, Bess?" she said. "That's fabulous. Do you get to talk?"

"Sort of," Bess said.

George looked at Nancy. She always looked at Nancy when she wanted a straight answer.

"Bess screams," Nancy said.

"Oh, yes, I've heard her," George said. "You

should have heard the scream she delivered last week when she caught me trying on her new denim jacket."

Bess blushed and cleared her throat to change the subject. "Nancy, are you going to finish your dinner?"

Nancy shook her head. "I'm too full," she said, passing her plate over to Bess.

"Gristle Pie was never this tender at good old River Heights High," Bess said, digging in.

"George," Nancy asked, "did you hear any of the movie people talking about Fenley Place while you were catering today?"

"Not a syllable. Why?"

Nancy looked disappointed, but George's eyes sparkled with curiosity. "I knew you were working on a mystery, Nancy."

"How did you know?"

George laughed. "Oh, something about the way you stirred seven packets of sweetener into your iced tea told me your mind was elsewhere. What's going on?"

"It was incredible," Bess blurted out. "And *I* saw it first. There was ugly red smoke pouring out of the chimney of Fenley Place."

"Interesting," George said, leaning forward to get all the details.

Nancy filled George in, describing the day's mysterious events during Bess's audition for Hank Steinberg. And she told George how no answers had turned up when they checked out Fenley Place. If no one was home, Nancy wondered out

31

loud again, who set off the red smoke, and why was there a woman looking out the window?

George's face grew more serious the more she heard.

"If the movie people knew what we know about Fenley Place, they'd really freak out," George said. "The word around the set is—"

Nancy shook her head no to signal George to stop. "Not in front of Bess," Nancy said. "She's too upset already."

"Uh, Bess, go get us some dessert while I tell Nancy some stories that I know you don't want to hear."

"I'm on my way," Bess said, carrying her tray away.

"So what's the news?" Nancy said.

George dropped her voice. "The word around the set is that the movie is jinxed. One stunt man broke his leg jumping out of a tree. Now the other stunt guys are saying that Steinberg just wants good stunts and doesn't care about keeping people alive."

Nancy looked interested and puzzled. "I wonder what that has to do with the red smoke?" she said, more to herself than to George.

"I don't know, but listen to this. People have been talking about a bunch of props and equipment doing a disappearing act."

"Lost or stolen?" Nancy asked.

George shrugged. "I don't know. Also, Jenny Logan and Deck Burroughs were filming a fight scene, and Jenny was supposed to hit Deck with a chair."

"Oh, right. A stunt chair," Nancy said. "I've seen them. They're made out of balsa wood and—"

"Correct. But Jenny hit him with a real chair by mistake. It knocked Deck cold. Jenny was scared to death. She thought she'd killed him or something. And Hank Steinberg blew up. He's convinced that someone is trying to sabotage his film."

It was all good information. But as far as Nancy could tell, none of it seemed to directly connect with the mystery at Fenley Place.

"I hope the Teppingtons get home soon." She sighed.

Bess returned with a tray of desserts. "Are you through?" she asked.

George nodded.

"Well, you've convinced me *not* to be a screamer," Bess said. "It sounds too dangerous."

"What do you mean? You didn't hear any of the stories," George said.

"No, but I watched Nancy's face from across the room," Bess said.

"Listen, Bess, don't quit the movie. There's nothing to be afraid of, believe me. Nothing's going to happen to you."

Just then all of the lights in The Schoolyard went out.

Bess screamed.

4

Lights! Camera! Explosion!

"Bess?" Nancy said, reaching across the table in the darkness for her frightened friend. But her hand grabbed air. Bess was gone!

Nancy stood up quickly. "Bess," she said louder.

"Nancy?" It was George's voice but it sounded distant and behind her.

Nancy took a step and bumped hard into something. "Sorry," she apologized but it turned out to be a chair. "Bess! George!"

Other voices were calling in the blacked-out restaurant. Chairs were falling, plates crashed onto the floor. Everyone seemed to be trying to find a way to the door.

It was too dark to see clearly, so Nancy inched toward where she thought the exit was.

But the confusion led everyone in circles. People were shouting, "Ouch—get off my foot!" or "Ooof —get out of my way."

Bodies bounced on all sides of her like bumper cars at an amusement park. Suddenly Nancy sensed someone was standing very close to her.

"Bess? George?"

Suddenly, two rough, callused hands wrapped themselves around her throat. Immediately, Nancy grabbed at the hands and pried them away from her neck. Then someone next to her screamed.

"Hahahahaha," laughed a deep voice.

"Mark Donaldson, get your hands off my throat! That's not funny!" a young woman yelled. Nancy recognized the voice as Sherrie Crocker, an acquaintance from high school. Mark, well-known at school as the class clown, kept laughing and, from the screams that followed, Nancy could tell that he was continuing to "strangle" people in the dark.

"Ouch!" cried a familiar voice behind her.

Nancy whirled around in the other direction. "Bess?"

"Nancy," Bess said, holding on to her friend. "I can't find George."

"We'll find her outside," Nancy said. "Let's get out of here."

George was waiting outside in the warm, moonlit evening. She had already gotten the story from a police officer on his beat. Most of River Heights had been blacked out.

"Hank Steinberg strikes again," George said. "All their movie lights overloaded the power lines. But the police think the electricity will be back on in about an hour."

All the street lights were out too, but the police had turned on the headlights of their cars to help the crowds in the street see.

So for the next hour, diners ate by candlelight in The Schoolyard.

"The food tastes better when you don't have to look at it," George said.

Bess didn't laugh.

"After dinner I'm going back to the McCauley house," George said.

Bess choked on her dessert when she heard that.

"Hey, unlike some people around here, I work all day over hot steam trays," George said. "I've got to do my movie-star gazing at night."

"Count me out," Bess said. "I'm never going near Highland Avenue again."

"Are you really going to pass up fame and fortune, Bess?" asked George.

"*You* spend an hour standing in the deathly shadows of Fenley Place"—Bess wasn't faking her theatrical voice now—"and then tell me there's nothing to worry about."

"Well, *I'm* not afraid of Fenley Place." George shrugged. "And, anyway, I'll be across the street watching Hank Steinberg film an incredible special effects scene tonight. He's going to blow out all the windows of the McCauley house. Anyone coming with me?"

"I am," Nancy said. "I want to see that. And maybe the Teppingtons will be home. I want to ask them about the red smoke coming out of their chimney."

"I'll be somewhere else," Bess answered once and for all.

Nancy and George hung around until Bess spotted a group of friends who were walking home together in the pitch dark. Bess joined them, and then Nancy and George drove to the McCauley House. By the time they reached Highland Avenue, the electricity had come back on. Nancy and George could see lights shining inside houses on the avenue.

Fenley Place was still dark and unoccupied, so Nancy and George crept up as close as they could to the McCauley house to see what was going on.

But they couldn't get too close because more barricades had been added, to keep the spectators farther away. In fact, there were two lines of barricades stretching all the way across Highland Avenue, from the McCauley property to the beginning of Fenley Place, sealing off access to both houses. And tonight, the security people were really enforcing the rules.

Why the area was suddenly so off limits wasn't clear until Nancy overheard some guys talking about the exploding windows scene they were shooting. Even though the special effects crew had installed fake glass, Hank Steinberg wanted to make triply sure no one got hurt in the explosion.

Crewmen were in and out of the house like a parade of ants, setting small explosive charges to the insides of every window frame in the McCauley House. Then they attached miniature radio receivers to each charge. Now, with just one push of a button on a radio transmitter, all of the windows in the house could be blown out at the same time by remote control.

"The crew was grumbling at dinner," George told Nancy. "They usually shoot a scene like this near the end of the filming because it makes such a mess. But they have to shoot it tonight because it's supposed to rain next week."

"How long are they going to be in River Heights?" Nancy asked.

"Fifteen shooting days, I think," George said. "They'll do most of the interior stuff back in a Hollywood studio."

Nancy's eyes scanned the area. Maybe she'd see Jenny Logan, the star who was going to be in the scene. Or maybe she'd see a familiar face, like Chris Hitchcock or Brandon.

What caught her eye instead was an unexpected, shimmering, jumpy light. It was coming from inside Fenley Place!

At first Nancy thought it was another reflection from the movie lights bouncing off the McCauley house windows. But the way the light bobbed and darted convinced her that it was coming from inside. Maybe it was a flashlight. If it was, that meant that someone was inside the house!

She tapped George on the arm and pointed across to Fenley Place. George saw the light, too.

"I'm going over there," Nancy said.

"I'll come with you," her friend volunteered.

But when they reached the end of the barricade, they ran into a security guard who didn't agree.

"Sorry, girls, you can't go through," said one of the guards.

"Why not?" asked George.

"Mr. Steinberg's orders," he said. "He doesn't want to take chances someone might get hurt. So this whole part of the street is off limits tonight."

"But we're just going into this house—Fenley Place," Nancy said. As she talked to the guard, she kept her eyes on the window where she'd seen the light. Right now it was dark.

"Do you live there?" asked the guard.

"No, but someone—"

He didn't give Nancy a chance to finish.

"If you don't live there, then you can't go through. Those are my orders."

"I get the feeling he's trying to tell us we can't go through," George said.

There was no other way to get to the house, because the barricades came right up to the wrought iron fence that surrounded the property.

"What about climbing the fence?" George asked Nancy.

"I thought about that," replied Nancy. "But, with those sharp spikes at the top, it would be impossible. Besides, I don't want to trespass on the neighbors' property."

So Nancy and George retreated. It seemed as if there was nothing they could do until after the scene was shot.

"This will just take a minute or two," George said. She sounded pleased with herself for having all the inside facts. "I heard that it isn't a very complicated scene. Jenny Logan runs out of the house and down the front lawn. While she's running, the windows explode behind her. That's all."

Relax, Nancy told herself. How long could it take to film that?

Jenny Logan sat on a tall director's chair, stretching her legs and relaxing her neck muscles. She was off to the side, by herself, but not entirely alone. A plump, ragged brown teddy bear was squeezed in the chair beside her. Even in just a plain white blouse and a short denim skirt, Jenny Logan looked beautiful. Her long straight blond hair seemed to glow in the moonlight.

Hank Steinberg came out of the McCauley house to direct the scene. He talked to Jenny for what seemed like a long time, showing her how he wanted her to run and how he wanted her to look.

The crowd of onlookers was packed so tightly around Nancy and George that they couldn't see Fenley Place clearly. But Nancy kept watching for the light again. At one point, she thought there was an eerie glow in the window to the left of the front door.

"If they would just shoot this thing and get it over with!" Nancy said impatiently. She knew that if there *was* someone in Fenley Place—a prowler— he wouldn't stick around all night.

"All right, let's do it!" Hank called from behind camera number one. It was positioned about thirty feet from the front door of the McCauley house.

He checked the five other cameras set up to catch the action at different angles. Three of them were aimed at the exploding windows, and two were set to follow Jenny.

Finally, Hank yelled "Action," and Jenny ran out

40

of the house as if something terrible were chasing her. It looked perfect, but the windows didn't explode. "Cut!" Hank called.

Time after time after time Jenny ran out of the house. But no matter how well she did it or how tired she seemed, Hank asked her to do it again.

"Hank," Jenny called out. Her soft voice with a trace of a southern accent was laced with tension. "When are you going to blow the windows?"

"When I'm ready, Jenny," Hank said sternly.

George groaned and Nancy glanced at Fenley Place. The light she had seen was out.

Again Jenny Logan came running out the front door. She looked a little more frantic, a little more frightened. Suddenly the windows exploded behind her with a tremendous noise that shook the ground.

Jenny's eyes went wild, and she screamed a horrible scream of genuine and utter surprise.

"Cut!" Hank shouted. "We got it, babe," he said as he went up to put his arm around Jenny.

"One of these days you're going to push me too far," Jenny said angrily.

Finally, the barricades opened, and Nancy and George made a dash for Fenley Place. But the house was dark. They rang the bell, they looked in the windows. The old house was cold, silent, and completely empty.

Early the next morning—too early for an ordinary call—the phone beside Nancy's bed jangled in her ear. She woke up and grabbed it quickly, so

41

that it wouldn't waken Hannah Gruen or her father.

"Hello?" The clock-radio on the nightstand said 5:00 A.M.

"Hello, Nancy? This is Sara Teppington." It was the familiar voice of Nancy's old high school English teacher. The same Sara Teppington who lived in Fenley Place.

"I'm sorry to call you so early," Mrs. Teppington said. "But I couldn't wait any longer. Please come to our house right now. Something terrible has happened."

5

Inside Fenley Place

Nancy was up, dressed, and out of the house before five-thirty. In her neighborhood, it was quiet because everyone was still sleeping. But when she got to Highland Avenue, there were at least five crew members already beginning to set up cables and rearrange lights. Still, the atmosphere was peaceful. And in the light of early dawn, Fenley Place didn't look so forbidding. At least from the outside. Sara Teppington, wearing a light blue running suit, greeted Nancy at the front door. Her long chestnut hair, which she always pinned up during school, was tied back, out of her face, in a ponytail.

"Thanks for coming, Nancy," she said, holding the door open so Nancy could step inside the house. The door creaked a little as it was closed.

Mrs. Teppington and Nancy stood for a moment in the small, dark entryway. Because of the low ceiling, being in the vestibule was like being in a box—or rather a coffin. The air felt close and tingly.

"How do you manage to look so good at this hour

of the morning?" said Mrs. Teppington with a smile. And without stopping for Nancy's answer she said, "If I look like I haven't gotten any sleep, it's because I haven't. We just got home about half an hour ago."

She walked Nancy into a den, yellow with early morning sun. Sara Teppington sat in a straight-backed antique rocker. Nancy sat on a soft old sofa.

"Is it too early for breakfast?" Mrs. Teppington said, pointing to a tray of croissants, butter and jam, and a pitcher of orange juice. "It looks great," Nancy said, pouring herself a glass of orange juice. "I ran out of the house pretty fast."

"I called you too early, didn't I?" In class Sara Teppington was the most patient listener of all the teachers in the school. But in her own home, she talked and moved in a faster rhythm. She didn't wait for Nancy to say anything before she spoke again.

"Last night, at about three A.M., four of the windows in this house exploded."

Nancy sat straight up on the sofa.

"We got a call from a neighbor who said that an explosion woke him up. He came outside and found broken glass all over the driveway. It's still there if you want to take a look."

"I will," Nancy said. "Do you have any idea what caused it?"

"No," Mrs. Teppington answered. "I want to find out what really happened, before I have to read a lot of ridiculous headlines about ghosts in Fenley Place. I thought maybe you could help. You did

44

such a good job when my computer was stolen at school."

Nancy looked around the room. It was cheerfully decorated, and yet there was still something unwelcoming about Fenley Place.

"I'd be glad to investigate for you," Nancy said. "But may I ask you a questions first? I always wondered how anyone could live in this house. Do you really like it?"

"It's a crazy old house. My husband hates it. My daughters hate it. And if our dog could speak, I'm sure he'd side with them. But Fenley Place and I understand each other." Her voice dropped to a whisper and she added, "We talk to each other."

Nancy smiled and whispered back, "Did it tell you why its windows exploded?"

"Maybe it would have if I'd been home," Sara Teppington said in a serious voice. "But we've been gone for a week."

"I know you weren't home yesterday afternoon," Nancy said.

"Yes, Mr. Titus told me you were here," said the teacher. "He's the one who called us last night. He's been keeping an eye on the house for us."

Slam!

The door to the den closed with a loud bang, and Nancy's legs twitched involuntarily.

"The breeze?" Nancy asked hopefully.

"The house knows we're talking about it," Sara Teppington said. Then she asked, "What were you doing here yesterday? Were you looking for me?"

45

"My friend and I saw red smoke coming out of your chimney yesterday."

Sara Teppington's face flinched the same way Nancy's face did when the door slammed. *"Our* chimney? How? No one was home."

She got up immediately and hurried to the living room. Nancy followed.

As Nancy and Mrs. Teppington approached the fireplace, two faces stared at them with hollow eyes. The faces were carved into either end of a smooth wooden mantel, and they both had expressions that were contorted, as if they were in pain. Nancy thought that Garver Fenley, the man who had built Fenley Place, must have been very strange.

A quick look confirmed that the fireplace hadn't been used at all recently. It had been swept clean. There were no ashes.

"See? Nothing's been burned here," Sara Teppington said.

Using a small flashlight from her purse, Nancy looked as far up the chimney as she could. "There's something kind of lumpy up near the top, but I can't tell what it is."

Sara Teppington got down on her hands and knees and looked up the chimney.

"It could be a bird's nest," she speculated. "I'll have my husband, Alan, check it out."

A cold breeze suddenly blew into the living room. "Let's go back to the den," Sara said, leading the way.

"Mrs. Teppington—"

"Call me Sara," the woman interrupted Nancy. "You're not my student anymore, Nancy, I'm sorry to say."

Nancy plopped back down on the sofa in the den and went on to tell Sara what else she had seen at Fenley Place.

"While I was investigating the smoke yesterday, I thought I saw a woman in a white nightgown, standing in a third-floor window. And last night, I came back to watch a scene of the movie being filmed."

Nancy paused for a minute. An idea suddenly flew into her head, but she couldn't get hold of it. She shrugged and continued her story. "And then I saw a light—it could have been a flashlight—flickering in your house."

Sara's brow furrowed, and for a moment she looked frightened. Then she just shook her head quickly.

"As far as we can tell nothing was stolen. Nothing was even moved around," Sara said. "Maybe there really *are* ghosts and they don't like my taste in interior decorating."

Their conversation was interrupted by a man's voice. "It's not a joke, Sara," he said. The two women turned to the door.

A tall man in a bulky, striped bathrobe was taking up most of the doorway. He had a bushy black beard, and his thick hair was equal parts of gray and black. He looked sleepy.

"A little early for a student conference, isn't it?" he asked.

"This is my husband, Alan," Mrs. Teppington said. "Alan, this is Nancy Drew. She's not my student. She's River Heights' best young detective."

"Of course," Alan Teppington said.

He didn't sound as though he believed it, or disbelieved it, either. He sounded as though he didn't care. He helped himself to some orange juice and then acted as if he were alone in the room.

"I shouldn't stay very long," Nancy said. "But I'd like to see where the windows exploded if you don't mind."

"Certainly. Come with me." Sara glared at her husband as she led Nancy out of the room. Alan followed.

The Teppingtons' bedroom was on the first floor near the back of the house. In it was one of the four windows that had exploded. Nancy could see that only the window pane had been destroyed, although there were small nicks and burn marks around the inside of the window frame. Sara explained that a few jagged pieces of glass had remained, but she had removed them. Now the hole was covered with heavy plastic, taped on all sides.

The other three windows, Sara said, were on the other side of the house, and they all looked the same.

"Can you think of anyone who'd want to do this to you?" Nancy asked.

"I own a book store," Alan Teppington said. "The only enemies I have are customers who browse but don't buy."

Nancy turned to Sara. "No," Sara said uncertainly. "Most of my students don't hold a grudge for very long."

"Are you saying that little jerk last year doesn't count, Sara?" Alan Teppington said, balling his hands into fists. "I wanted to push his face through a juicer after what he did."

"Alan, please," Sara said. She used her classroom tone and authority. But there was an additional plea in her voice for moderation. Apparently, moderation was a virtue Alan Teppington had never learned.

Nancy knew the "little jerk" Alan was talking about. It was Josh Petrie, a real hard case.

"Sara failed him last year," Alan Teppington said, glaring into Nancy's eyes. "And believe me, he got the grade he earned. But he wanted revenge. So one night he broke into our house and gave it a good going over with spray paint and glue. I don't know what it is with you kids."

"Josh Petrie is gone," Sara Teppington said firmly. "He joined the army a few months ago. He's not doing this."

"That's just what we need," Alan Teppington laughed sarcastically. "Josh Petrie defending this nation. *I* feel safer. How about you?"

Once again his eyes tried to drill through Nancy.

"Shh!" Nancy said.

It wasn't a scold. There were noises on the ceiling above them. Were they footsteps in the room above them?

"Is anyone else home?" Nancy asked:

"Yes, my daughters. But they're still asleep."

"Do you suppose I could see the room upstairs, since that's where I saw the woman standing yesterday?"

"There's a staircase at the back of the house," Sara Teppington said. "The room you're talking about is our attic."

The Teppingtons followed Nancy up a dark, narrow staircase to the third floor. They listened motionless, breathing the stale air as quietly as they could.

There was no one there. The sounds they had heard from downstairs were the uncomfortable creaking of the walls and floors of Fenley Place.

With her flashlight, Nancy made a sweep of the cobwebbed beams of the attic. Then she aimed it at the wide-planked dusty floor. Most of it was piled with boxes, crates, suitcases, stacks of old magazines, and old furniture. Everything had gathered dust by the inch, waiting to be of use or to be thrown out.

"Someone *has* been up here recently," Nancy said suddenly.

Alan Teppington sneezed loudly. "How do you know?" he asked impatiently.

Nancy knelt by a fresh footprint in the dusty floor. For a moment she studied the pattern of lines and circles the shoe's tread had made in the dust. "A running shoe, probably," she said.

She took a notebook from her purse and made a quick sketch of the shoe print.

"Alan, look at your trunk," Sara Teppington called out in surprise.

Nancy's flashlight quickly found what Sara Teppington was pointing at. It was a large black leather steamer trunk.

"What's wrong with it?" Nancy asked.

"I always keep it covered with one of my grandmother's old nightgowns," Sara Teppington said.

"A white nightgown?" Nancy asked.

Sara nodded.

A quick search through the attic revealed the white lace nightgown hanging on a coat tree.

Sara Teppington didn't know how it got there. And Nancy didn't know if this was the nightgown she had seen the woman wearing the day before.

"The girls were probably playing up here," Alan Teppington said.

But his wife contradicted him. "Amy and Kate know they aren't allowed to play in the attic, and I don't believe they'd break that rule."

Nancy went farther into the attic for a closer look at the black leather trunk. She rubbed her finger across gold initials in the leather—A.T., Alan Teppington. She knew there was only one reason why the trunk wasn't dusty.

"Mr. Teppington, someone has probably been rummaging through your trunk," Nancy said.

Mr. Teppington kicked a stack of cardboard boxes. "Well, then, I've got a clue for you," he said, shaking his head. "Just go out and look for a thief who's a complete idiot. Because there's nothing in my trunk except old clothes that don't fit and memories I don't think about."

Alan Teppington must have the world's shortest temper, Nancy thought. So she asked him as calmly as she could to check through his trunk, "just to see if anything is missing."

Alan Teppington grabbed the flashlight from Nancy's hand and made a quick search of his trunk.

"They didn't take anything, okay?"

"Alan, don't be rude. Nancy is trying to help."

"We don't need a detective. We need a real estate agent. We need to get out of this house and go somewhere where your crazy students and wise-guy movie location flunkies and teenage girl detectives don't bother us!"

He turned to go down the attic stairs but there were little footsteps coming up in a hurry.

The Teppington daughters, Amy, age five, and Kate, age ten, ran up the stairs in their nightgowns. "Mommy!" they screamed. Their faces were red from crying and tears streamed down their cheeks.

Alan stooped down, put his arms around both girls, and tried to hold them tightly. But they began sobbing harder and hitting their father with their fists.

6

Where Is Boris?

Between sobs, the Teppington girls were saying, "You hate Boris! He's gone and it's all your fault!"

"Girls," Alan Teppington called, trying to get their attention. "I didn't do anything to that rotten dog."

"You said last night you were going to get rid of him!" Amy said, whistling slightly through two missing front teeth.

"Calm down, girls," their mother ordered. "Your father would never hurt Boris."

"But, Mom, we've looked everywhere," Kate said. "We can't find him. Boris is gone!"

The girls ran to their mother, sobbing the dog's name.

Watching Amy and Kate cry in their mother's comforting arms, Alan Teppington seemed to melt inside his oversized bathrobe.

"Girls," he said several times in a very quiet voice. When they had cried all they could, they became quiet enough to listen to him. "Amy,

Kate," their father said softly, "I *was* very angry with Boris yesterday."

"You've been very angry about everything, Daddy," Kate said with schoolteacher authority.

"Yes," he said. He ran his hand through his thick, bushy hair and tightened the belt on his robe. "But last night, after you were in bed, Boris and I had a heart-to-heart talk. He agreed not to chew up any more of my paperbacks and I agreed not to eat any of his dog biscuits."

Kate actually giggled at that point, but her younger sister asked seriously, "But where is he now, Daddy?"

"I don't know," Alan Teppington said. Then his eyes fell on Nancy, standing in the attic shadows. Suddenly he seemed very happy that she was there.

"Girls, this is Nancy Drew," Alan Teppington said, pulling Nancy toward his daughters. "And you know what? Nancy is great at finding things, aren't you, Nancy?"

Nancy bent down on her knees to be closer to the two sniffling girls. "I'm terrific at it," she said with a smile. "I bet I can find Boris. But I'll need some help from you two."

The two little girls looked at the young detective for a moment, examining her face carefully.

"First of all," Nancy said. "What does Boris look like?"

"He's the most beautiful dog in the world," Amy said seriously.

Nancy looked up at the girls' mother. Sara

54

grinned and said, "He's part bassett hound, part beagle, part something else. He's medium height, has got a heavy build, and short hair."

"Okay, here's my plan," Nancy said. "Kate and Amy, you come with me, and we'll cover the neighborhood on foot."

"I want to take my bike," Amy said.

"Okay. Kate and I will cover the neighborhood on foot and Amy will ride her bike," Nancy said. "Agreed?" The girls nodded.

"Thank you, Nancy," Sara said. "That way Alan and I can make a wider circle in the car."

"Great," said Nancy.

"Well, let's get dressed, everybody!" Alan Teppington ordered.

His voice was a starter's pistol for Amy and Kate. They went running downstairs.

After the children were gone, Alan Teppington said, "Thanks for helping out, Nancy. It's true that I hate that dog, but my kids mean everything to me."

Nancy smiled. She didn't mind helping out, especially if it meant getting out of the clammy atmosphere of Fenley Place and into the fresh air.

For the next hour, Nancy, Kate, and Amy went up and down all the side streets between Highland Avenue and the street behind it. They looked and called for Boris, stopping at every yard.

But none of the neighbors had seen Boris that morning. And many said they had never seen Boris ever—which was true.

Boris didn't circulate much. Amy explained that even when he was left alone outside, he would never leave the Teppingtons' property.

"Mom says it's because he's always protecting us," Kate explained.

"Daddy says it's because Boris never wants to leave his food bowl," Amy said. "Daddy's funny when he's not yelling."

"I noticed," Nancy said cautiously.

"I don't know why, but he's been really tense lately. Ever since that movie crew took over the McCauley house," Kate said.

When they took shortcuts through backyards, Amy walked her bike.

"Why doesn't your dad like movie people?" Nancy asked.

"They're phony and selfish," Amy said in exactly her father's tone of voice.

Kate added, "He said we could go across the street and watch them, but a day later he told us to get in the car and we went to that country inn. I don't get it, do you?"

"Not yet," Nancy said.

They looked everywhere for Boris. They even checked at the McCauley house. By now the crew was setting up for another stunt. There was a lot of activity on the roof. But Boris was nowhere in sight.

Before giving up, they tried one more place. Pat Ellis's Elegant Eats had set up a large catering tent in the tiny park at the end of Highland Avenue. The movie people could sit on the grass or at long tables and enjoy everything from a cup of coffee to a five-course breakfast.

Nancy and the girls wandered into the park and found George stationed at a serving table filled with food.

George waved.

"These are Amy and Kate, *Mrs. Teppington's* daughters," Nancy said. "We're looking for their dog, Boris." She described Boris to George.

"And his tongue hangs out of the left side of his mouth," added Kate.

"Sounds like a guy who was hanging around the pecan buns," George said, laughing. "But seriously, I haven't seen any *real* animals around here today. Sorry. What kind of dog is he?"

"He's just a brown mutt," Kate said affectionately.

George's eyes shifted to a coffee urn that was bubbling for attention in the corner. "I'll watch for him," she said. "Gotta run, guys. Hope you find your dog."

Nancy led the girls back toward their house.

"Maybe spacemen came down and took Boris for a ride in their spaceship," Amy said.

"If they did, they'll be sorry," Kate said.

"Why?" asked Nancy.

"Boris throws up a lot in the car."

The girls watched their parents' car pull into their driveway. They ran home, hoping to find a fuzzy face hanging out the back window. But they were disappointed.

"No luck, girls," their mother said.

"We didn't find him, either," Kate said.

Nancy could see that Amy was getting ready to cry again. "This means we've got to put plan B into action," Nancy said quickly.

"What's plan B?" asked Amy.

"Missing dog posters," Nancy explained. And she gave out assignments. "Amy, you draw a picture of Boris. Kate will write his description and all the other important information on the poster. Then your mom can get it photocopied, and you can put the copies up all over the neighborhood."

The two girls went into the house to work on plan B.

"That dog didn't run away," Alan Teppington said. "He'd never leave those kids."

"Alan thinks someone stole the dog," Sara Teppington said. "Well, I'm going in the house to call the pound, in case someone turns him in."

"Thanks again, Nancy, for your help," Alan said. "I wish I could pay you back somehow."

"As a matter of fact, Mr. Teppington, there is one thing you could do."

"What?"

"Could you climb up on the roof and check out the chimney? I think there's something in there and maybe it has something to do with the red smoke. Did Mrs. Teppington tell you about that?"

Alan Teppington nodded abruptly. Then he dragged out a long expandable ladder from the garage. He hauled it to the side of the house and planted it firmly in the ground. After raising the ladder as high as it would go, he climbed to the roof and disappeared.

Nancy walked around to the front of the house to see him better.

He was a big man and not graceful, but he walked the roof confidently. He walked with his feet straddling the crest of the roof and his arms outstretched like a tightrope walker.

A little farther, a little farther. Nancy coached him silently.

There was a loud crash at the side of the house. It made Nancy jump, and she took her eyes off the roof for just a second.

Alan Teppington instinctively looked behind him to see what had caused the noise. In that instant, he lost his balance. With a yell, he started rolling down the slope of the roof.

When Nancy looked up she saw him heading helplessly for the edge of the roof—and a three-story fall onto the sharp spikes of the wrought-iron fence below.

7

Double Horror

"No!" Alan Teppington shouted. He was almost to the edge of the roof.

Nancy stood, frozen in horror, holding her breath. There was nothing she could do. Maybe he could grab on to the gutter before he fell, but it would never hold a man his size.

At the last possible second, Alan Teppington stretched out his arms and grabbed a thin tree branch that just barely overhung the roof of the house. It stopped him from rolling, and he lay, face down and motionless, right at the edge of the roof.

Nancy rushed to the side of the house to climb the ladder. But it was no longer standing against the house. It was lying on the ground.

So that was the crash she and Alan had heard!

Using all her strength, Nancy tried to lift up the ladder and stand it against the house, but it was too tall and heavy; it was like trying to lift a fallen tree.

From the front of the house, Sara Teppington's voice cried out in sudden terror. "Alan!" she shouted. And then in a more quiet voice she coaxed, "Don't move. Just don't move."

Nancy was still struggling with the ladder, when a new voice came up behind her and said, "Let me help you, little lady."

She turned to find that the Texas drawl belonged to a bald man in faded jeans and a Western-cut checked shirt.

As soon as the ladder was steady again, the man bounded up the steps shouting, "Hold on there, fella. I'm on my way!"

Nancy watched anxiously from the ground and kept her hands on the ladder to make sure it didn't fall again.

Finally, Alan Teppington started climbing down with the other man's help. Alan's face was as white as the old nightgown in his attic. His hands and nose were scraped and skinned red from the roof shingles.

Once the two of them were back on the ground, the man introduced himself as Dallas Cranshaw. "I'm a grip over on the movie set," he said, with a friendly grin. "I was setting up a camera when I happened to look over here and see what happened."

Sara Teppington came running out the back door.

"What happened?" she asked breathlessly. "Alan, you're bleeding."

"Your husband forgot where the diving board was, that's all," Dallas said, still wearing his grin. "You know, fella, next time you oughta plant that ladder real good so it won't fall."

Alan Teppington's eyebrows came together in a tight scowl. "I planted that ladder halfway to China!"

"He did. I saw him," Nancy said.

The flush of anger once again filled Alan Teppington's face. "The only way that ladder could have fallen is if someone *pushed* it over." He glared accusingly at Dallas.

"Alan, what were you doing up on the roof, anyway?" Sara asked.

Nancy answered, reminding Sara that they both wanted to know what the lump in the chimney was.

"Did you find out?" Sara asked.

Alan shook his head no.

"Come into the house and let me patch you up," Sara coaxed her husband.

"I'm telling you, someone pushed that ladder," were Alan's final words.

Nancy turned her attention to Dallas Cranshaw when the Teppingtons had gone.

"It was lucky you were watching," Nancy said. "Did you happen to see how the ladder fell?"

"I didn't see anybody," Dallas answered. "But I'll tell you this: that house is more jinxed than this movie we're working on."

"What makes you say that?"

"It gives me the jitters just to *think* about it," Dallas replied. "But do you know what happened while we were filming up there on the roof this morning?" He pointed to the McCauley house. Nancy shook her head.

"A stunt man walked around on the roof, got

scared, and fell off," Dallas said. "Of course, our guy had a big old mattress to fall into. Makes a difference."

Dallas looked at Fenley Place with a cautious eye. "If I was them, I'd leave, that's what I'd do."

"Oh, I think you're overreacting a little bit," Nancy said.

Dallas shook his head slowly. "I *saw* that red smoke, little lady. First the smoke, then the windows, and now this. I tell you, it's like everything we do at the McCauley house—or plan on doing—happens *for real* at Fenley Place!"

Suddenly Nancy felt as though she couldn't move. The idea that had flown out of her head in the Teppington's den flew back again. Dallas was right—everything they filmed for the movie script had been repeated at Fenley Place. A big knot formed in her stomach as she asked herself a single question: What was going to happen next?

Dallas started walking away and then he noticed that Nancy was still standing in the same spot, staring off into space. He looked back with his head cocked to one side. "Hey—I didn't mean to scare you," he said.

"Just tell me one thing," Nancy said very slowly. "Is there by any chance a dog in that movie?"

Dallas gave a nod.

"What happens to him?"

"He's found dead in front of the fireplace. Why?"

Nancy could feel the knot move from her stomach into her chest.

"Dallas," she said, "I've got to get a look at the *Terror Weekend* script."

"Are you kidding?" Dallas said with a laugh. "Hank Steinberg wouldn't show a script to his own mother until after the movie was filmed and cut."

"I don't care," Nancy said. "He's got to make an exception for me. The Teppingtons could be in a lot of trouble, if someone is trying to make them live out every scene from the movie. And I know you'd blame yourself, Dallas, if anything really awful happened—wouldn't you?"

Dallas chewed on his lower lip. He was doing some serious thinking.

"Well, I'll let you see my copy, but if somebody catches you with it, you don't know where you got it. Okay?"

"Got what?" Nancy said, smiling.

A few minutes later, Nancy was sitting on the ground, resting her back against an old maple tree in the park at the end of Highland Avenue. In her lap was a thick ring binder. The label on the cover said *"Terror Weekend."*

Inside were pages of many different colors: white, blue, green, pink, yellow, tan—a different color paper had been used each time a page of script was changed or rewritten. The final script, a shooting script Dallas called it, looked like a rainbow. By using this colored-paper system, people talking about a scene would know they were talking about the most recent revision.

As Nancy read the script her pulse began to race, just as if she were watching the movie in a theater.

Terror Weekend was about a house that turned against its inhabitants. Furniture would fly around the room almost crushing the family. Bloodred smoke poured out of the chimney, and the windows exploded. Phones would ring incessantly—even when they were off the hook—until the family nearly went crazy. The walls of a room closed in on a little girl. When she read that part, Nancy immediately worried about Kate and Amy.

And then there was the dead dog.

The worst of course was saved for the end of the movie. In the middle of the night, when everyone in the family was finally safe and sound asleep, the house spontaneously caught fire and burned to the ground.

There was a handwritten note on the final script page. It read, "Ending: Did the family get out?" The answer, written in a different handwriting, said, "To be determined by Hank on location."

8

Boris Is Found

Nancy closed the book.

How could she tell the Teppingtons about this script? She didn't want to frighten them, especially not Amy and Kate. But she couldn't just let them stay at Fenley Place without warning them about what might happen.

Nancy returned the script to Dallas with thanks. Then she stopped in at Fenley Place to see how Alan Teppington was. She also wanted to give her father a call to ask if he needed her to run some errands that afternoon. Sara was only too happy to let Nancy use the phone.

After speaking to her father, Nancy joined Sara in the den. "How is Mr. Teppington feeling?" she asked.

"He's behind the garage shooting jump shots," Sara said. "He does that when he's *really* upset. Kate and Amy are working on the missing dog poster. I don't think they even know their father almost broke his neck."

"Good," Nancy said. "Listen, I've got to run

some errands for my dad, but I'll be back later, after dinner. I need to talk to you."

The teacher brushed a wisp of hair from her forehead. "I don't get it, do you?" Sara Teppington said.

"I'm starting to," Nancy said.

After a quick lunch at a fast-food restaurant, Nancy started her errands. The list was a long one, and it took Nancy all afternoon to complete most of her tasks. Now it was getting late in the day. But just the same, in between picking up an envelope at the courthouse and a get-well card for one of her father's associates, Nancy couldn't resist doing an errand for herself.

She parked her car in front of Wishing Wells Shoe Shop and put a coin in the meter.

"Nancy," cried Mrs. Wells excitedly, when Nancy entered the shop. "I've got a brand new shoe, and it has your name written all over it."

Mrs. Wells showed Nancy a black pump. Amazingly, it did have the word *Nancy* written all over it in different colors of glittering ink.

"It's called the Ego Tripper," Mrs. Wells said. "Twenty-six different names in all the popular sizes."

"I'll think about it, Mrs. Wells," Nancy said.

Then Nancy took out the sketch of the footprint she had made in the Teppingtons' attic. "Do you sell a running shoe with this pattern on the sole?"

"Oh, my," Mrs. Wells said. "I've never seen anything like that."

"Well, I hope you won't mind if I look around," Nancy said. She went directly to the display of running shoes and turned over shoe after shoe, looking at the treads. Finally, one shoe matched the print of her sketch. It was called the Pacer, and it was manufactured by Killer Shoes, Los Angeles, California.

"Found it!" Nancy called triumphantly.

"Oh, good," Mrs. Wells replied. "Do you want to try them on?"

Nancy looked at the price tag on the bottom of the shoe and almost gasped. It was the most expensive running shoe she had ever seen.

"No thanks," she told Mrs. Wells. She put the sketch away and headed for the door.

"But, Nancy, what do you think about the Ego Tripper?"

"Unforgettable, Mrs. Wells. I mean it."

It was almost dinnertime, so Nancy made a quick stop at a card store nearby. Then she hopped into her car and headed home.

Okay, she thought as she drove, find the feet wearing a pair of Pacers and you'll find the visitor in the Teppingtons' attic. All of a sudden, she realized she should have looked for footprints around the ladder.

That would have to wait until after dinner, where the guest of honor was scheduled to be Bob Seglow, one of Carson Drew's old college friends.

Nancy arrived home and found her father involved in one of his favorite activities: teasing Hannah Gruen while she cooked a special dinner.

"I don't know, Hannah," Carson Drew said, his eyes twinkling. "This gravy doesn't look dark enough to me."

"You know perfectly well that those are the mashed potatoes," Hannah Gruen said. "Can't you get him out of here, Nancy?"

Carson Drew walked with his daughter out of the kitchen, through the dining room, and into his study.

"Where have you been all day?" he asked.

"Fenley Place," Nancy said. She told her father about the windows blowing out, the clues she found in the attic, and Alan Teppington's near-plunge from the roof. Then she described how Dallas had come to the rescue by letting her read the script. Finally, she told him how she found the shoe that matched the print.

Nancy gave her father a triumphant look. And he smiled at how much she looked like her mother at that moment.

"Busy day," said the lawyer. "Well, remember, my old friend Bob Seglow just happens to be the chief sound technician on Hank Steinberg's crew."

"He is?"

Carson Drew beamed at his little surprise, and Nancy gave her father a hug. Now she would really have an inside track on who might be causing the trouble at Fenley Place.

At dinner that evening, Bob Seglow sat at the end of the table in the guest of honor seat, telling fascinating stories about the movies he had worked on. He had a short haircut, a long mustache, and a

69

few pounds to lose. Nancy liked the casual but confident way he dressed: he wore jeans, a blue work shirt, and a sweater tied around his neck.

Bess and George, who had been invited to dinner, listened attentively to Bob's stories. Nancy tried to get her questions in edgewise, but it was hard. Each time she asked something, Bob would launch into another twenty-minute anecdote full of fabulous bits of inside Hollywood information.

In the middle of one story, Nancy received a phone call. It was Kate Teppington, Sara's ten-year-old daughter. She was still worried about her missing dog.

"Well, did you put up the posters?" Nancy asked Kate.

"Yes. But Boris isn't home yet."

Nancy's stomach turned over with fear, but she managed to keep any apprehension she felt out of her voice. "Kate, you've got to wait for people to see the posters. Someone will find him soon."

There was a quiet but disappointed "okay" on the other end of the line and then a dial tone.

Nancy came back to the dining room and apologized for the interruption.

"Where was I?" Bob Seglow asked.

Bess spoke up.

"You were telling us how Spider Hutchings got the job as stunt man for Hank Steinberg," she said, her blue eyes wide with anticipation. "He was scaling the outside of a building in downtown Los Angeles . . ."

"Right," Bob Seglow picked up the story again. "So Spider climbs all the way up to the tenth floor because that's where Hank Steinberg's office is. And Hank is having a big meeting.

"So Spider knocks on the window, and people look over and they see a guy outside the window on the tenth floor. *No scaffolding!* Three secretaries and two of the producers pass out immediately. But someone unlocks the window and Spider climbs in.

"'Hey, I hear you're looking for stunt men,' Spider says to Hank.

"Hank doesn't know what's going on, but he's trying to act like he's in control. So he says, 'Not today.'"

"Then what happened?" Bess asked.

"This is what Spider Hutchings is made of," Bob Seglow said. "He says 'okay,' opens the window again, and jumps out."

Everyone at the table gasped.

"Well," Bob said, "those who could still walk—Hank Steinberg among them—run to the window and look down. But Spider had set up a net under the window. He's lying there looking up at them like a baby in a cradle. Hank can't resist. He hires Spider on the spot."

Nancy listened and laughed along with everyone else. But the story had reminded her of an important question: whose footprints were in the attic?

"Mr. Seglow," Nancy asked, "a man like Spider Hutchings could climb into an attic window without a ladder, couldn't he?"

71

"That man could climb anywhere anytime," Bob Seglow said. "Especially if there's a practical joke at the other end."

After the long and story-filled dinner, Carson Drew and Bob Seglow excused themselves and went into Mr. Drew's den, where they planned to look at their college yearbook.

George had to get to bed early, since she was working at 5:30 the next morning. So she thanked Hannah for dinner and said goodnight. When Bess heard that Nancy was planning to go back to Fenley Place soon, she decided to head home, too.

So Nancy was left alone to figure out just what exactly she should tell the Teppingtons about the movie script she'd read. On the way to their house, she pondered the possibilities.

Was it possible, for instance, that the red smoke in their chimney and the red smoke in the script were not connected? Or the instant replay of the exploding window scene? Not really, Nancy decided. There were too many strange similarities between the script and the recent events at Fenley Place.

As Nancy approached the mysterious old house, she saw Alan and Sara Teppington sitting on the front lawn with their arms around each other. They were watching the stars—not the movie stars across the street from their house, but the clear black summer sky, which looked paint spattered with yellow and white dots.

"Good news," Nancy said. Her voice startled them.

"Oh, hi, Nancy," Sara said sleepily. "What's the good news?"

"I know what kind of shoe left the print in your attic."

"But do you know who was wearing the shoe?" asked Alan Teppington. "That's what counts."

"Not yet, but I'm going to work on that tonight," Nancy said. "But first, there's something I'd better tell you."

Just then a frightened child's scream came bursting from Fenley Place behind them.

"That was Amy!" Sara cried out.

She and her husband both jumped to their feet just as Amy came running out the front door and down the lawn. She was crying and screaming.

"What is it? What's wrong?" her mother asked, holding her daughter's shoulders tightly.

Over and over again, Amy sobbed the answer.

"Boris is dead!" she cried.

9

Spider Hutchings

Amy collapsed, sobbing, into her mother's enfolding arms.

"You were dreaming, sweetie," Sara said, stroking Amy's long brown hair.

"No, no, no, no, no!" Amy said, shaking her head violently. "I saw him. He's dead."

"Where?" Sara asked.

"In front of the fireplace," Nancy Drew answered.

Sara Teppington turned and shot a questioning look at Nancy. Then Amy struggled away from her mother and ran back toward the house. Sara, Alan, and Nancy followed her.

When they reached the living room, they stopped in the doorway.

There, on the floor in front of the carved wooden fireplace, lay the stiff, unmoving body of Boris.

For a moment, the adults were frozen, as motionless as the dog. Then Alan went forward and knelt down, resting a hand on the dog's side.

"Shhhh," he said looking up at Sara and Nancy. "I think he's breathing. He's still alive."

Quickly he lifted the limp, heavy animal into his arms and carried Boris out to their station wagon.

"I want to go with you, Daddy," Amy pleaded.

"All right," Alan replied. "Sara—call the vet and tell him we're on our way. I don't think we should wake up Kate now. We'll tell her about Boris in the morning.

His wife nodded in agreement.

Nancy waited in the den while Sara made the phone call and then poured two glasses of iced tea. In the morning, the room had seemed like the safest, friendliest spot in Fenley Place. But at night the old-fashioned kerosene globe lamp cast huge shadows on the curtains and walls.

"Now." Sara said just that one word as she settled herself into the rocking chair. When Nancy didn't begin speaking right away, Sara said sternly, "How did you know that Boris would be in front of the fireplace?"

"It's in the script," Nancy said simply.

"What script?"

"I read the script of *Terror Weekend* today," Nancy said. "The red smoke, the exploding windows, *and* the dead dog—they're all in the script. I know it sounds weird but it's like there are two horror movies being made—the one at the McCauley house, and the one at Fenley Place."

Sara shook her head and looked hurt.

"Why would anyone on the movie crew want to duplicate those things at our house?" she said.

"I don't know," Nancy said. "Do you or your husband know any of the movie people personally?"

"No. We haven't even talked to any of them except that boy, Chris Hitchcock, and Hank Steinberg. They both came over quite a few times, oh, it must have been two months ago. They wanted to film here, but Alan hates Hollywood people and he wouldn't hear of it."

"I know," Nancy said. "Kate and Amy told me how he feels." She cleared her throat before asking the next question. "I hope you won't take this the wrong way but, was your husband rude to Hank Steinberg? I mean, would Mr. Steinberg have a reason to hold a grudge?"

"You've seen how Alan can be." Sara gave a smile of both apology and tolerance for her husband's behavior. "I can't say he was on his best behavior with Hank."

"Well," Nancy said, "I'll check it out. Meanwhile, I just thought you'd better know about some of the other things in the script."

Nancy described the worst parts of *Terror Weekend*, including the ending, when the house burns to the ground.

"I guess this means we can cross Josh Petrie off the list as a suspect," Sara said. "Not only is he in the army, but he has nothing to do with the movie production company."

"True," Nancy agreed. "I think whoever is terrorizing your family must be connected with the film."

"I almost don't want to ask this," Sara said. "But what's going to happen next? In the script, I mean."

"They don't shoot the scenes in order," Nancy answered, "so I don't know. I'll try to find out. And maybe tomorrow, you should talk to Hank Steinberg yourself, to let him know what's happening here—although I think he may already know. Rumors circulate pretty fast."

"I wish Alan would come home," Sara said.

Sara Teppington got her wish. The station wagon was heard in the driveway, and a few minutes later Alan walked in, carrying Amy instead of the dog.

"Talk softly, she just fell asleep," he told his wife. "The vet kept Boris, but he's going to be all right. He was drugged, tranquilized somehow. We can pick him up in the morning."

"I've got to be going," Nancy said quickly. She wanted to leave *before* Sara told Alan the latest news. She didn't want to be there for another of his explosions. "I'll call you tomorrow if there's anything new to report."

Outside, the night was clear and cool. It felt so good to Nancy to have some open space and some fresh air to breathe. Highland Avenue was bustling with movie crew people setting up for some exterior nighttime shots.

Since it was getting late, the crowd of spectators had dwindled, and so the security lines had eased up. Nancy found she was able to move around through the jungle of lights, trucks, and equipment pretty freely.

She was just about to thread her way through the

maze, to search for Spider Hutchings, when she saw a familiar form standing on the outskirts of the action.

"Bess?" Nancy came up behind the spectator and caught her by surprise.

"Hi! Am I glad to see you!" Bess said.

Nancy smiled. "What are you doing here? I thought you gave up fame and fortune because you didn't dare come within ten blocks of Fenley Place."

"I almost did. But then I said to myself: 'Be brave, Bess Marvin. Where else can you make good money just for doing one scream?' And anyway, I really want to be in the movie. So I decided to try coming here tonight, and if I don't think about Fenley Place and get too scared, I'm coming back tomorrow."

"Great," Nancy said. "Well, I'm going to look around a bit. Do you want to come with me?" Nancy tried to sound casual. She knew if Bess heard about Boris and the other recent troubles at Fenley Place, she might lose her new-found nerve.

"Who are you investigating?" Bess asked.

"Spider Hutchings," Nancy said.

Bess was surprised. Spider had sounded like a wild and exciting guy according to Bob Seglow's stories. "Do you think Spider Hutchings planted the red smoke in the chimney?" Bess asked.

"I'll tell you after I look at his shoes," said Nancy.

Nancy and Bess walked past the crew and onto the lawn of the McCauley house. One of the

78

security guards waved them on, calling out, "Hiya, Screamer!"

"You're getting to be a real celebrity around here," Nancy said to Bess.

Passing the front porch of the McCauley house, Bess went up for a quick peek in the windows.

"Deck Burroughs and Jenny Logan are sitting in directors' chairs," Bess announced to Nancy. "There's Hank Steinberg. And Chris Hitchcock."

Nancy climbed the steps to the porch and peeked in the window too. Everything was just as Bess had described it—except for one horrible detail. Lying in front of the fireplace was the limp, motionless body of a dog.

Nancy walked off the porch, her stomach fluttery. "We've got to hurry," she said.

They walked into the backyard of the McCauley house and found two crew men setting up a bright spotlight by a tall oak tree.

"Have you seen Spider Hutchings?" Nancy asked.

One of the men pointed—straight up. "Spider," he called. "Visitors. Pretty ones."

Suddenly the top branches of the oak tree fluttered and snapped and something came swooping down. It was Spider Hutchings, making his entrance, swinging down from the top of the tree on a rope.

Before he even looked at Nancy and Bess, Spider said to the other men, "Tell Hank the rope's fine but the tree's not high enough."

"Maybe we can come back in ten years. It'll be

taller then," joked a man with a toothpick in his mouth.

Spider's laugh almost shook the leaves off the tree. Finally, he turned to Nancy and Bess.

In the flesh, Spider was just as Bob Seglow had described him—almost larger than life. He was six feet tall, muscular, and red-haired.

"Hi," he said. "What can I do for you?"

"Could I get a look at your shoes?" Nancy said.

"Usually people want to see a stunt man's scars," Spider said.

"Fans get stranger every day," the man with the toothpick joked.

Spider laughed again. "Hey, I've got a scar that's a perfect horse's hoof," he said. "Got it in a Western when I fell off a horse and it decided to do a little tap dance on my back. Want to see?"

"I really am more interested in your shoes," Nancy said.

So Spider lifted his right leg into the light and showed off his brand new pair of running shoes. It was the Pacer—the shoe Nancy was looking for.

"Nice," Nancy said. "Do you wear those all the time, or only to climb trees?"

"I just got them a couple of days ago," Spider said. "I'm trying them out for stunt work, and then we'll see. Why?"

"Could you climb something like the wall of a house wearing those shoes?" Nancy asked.

"I guess, but I'd look like a cat trying to climb a greased tree," Spider said with a laugh. He was about to give Bess a slap on the back but he stopped himself just in time. "I wear spiked boots for building work. Listen, do you have a reason for being so nosy?"

"Yes," Nancy said, "but I'd rather not tell you what it is just yet."

Nancy asked him what they'd be filming the next day, but Spider said he didn't know.

"Hank keeps changing his mind. Makes it kind of hard to prepare for my stunts, if you know what I mean." Spider sounded disgusted, but he shrugged his shoulders as if to say it was no big deal.

"Ask Hank Steinberg," Spider called out as Nancy and Bess walked back toward the street. "He's the man holding the reins and cracking the whip."

Nancy had already decided it was time to talk to Hank Steinberg. She and Bess stationed themselves near Hank Steinberg's personal trailer. They hoped to catch him there when he wasn't too busy.

It was close to midnight when Hank Steinberg came walking briskly toward his trailer. Assistants trailed behind him like the tail of a comet.

"Mr. Steinberg?" Nancy said.

The director immediately turned toward them. "It's the screamer and her friend, isn't it?" he said, stopping before he climbed the trailer steps. "What can I do for you?"

"I'd like to talk to you about Fenley Place," Nancy said. "Do you have a minute?"

Hank Steinberg looked at her with a puzzled

expression. "Detective dialogue out of a teenage girl's mouth. I think there's a movie idea in it," he said.

Bess giggled, and Nancy could feel her face turning red.

"I'll call it *The Blushing Detective*—just a working title, of course," Hank Steinberg said. "But seriously, please come in and tell me what's on your mind."

He opened the door and motioned Nancy and Bess inside. The trailer was a mess. On one side, chairs were piled high with movie posters, script pages, and movie industry newspapers.

The other side of the trailer was filled with games: the newest computer games, the oldest board games, mechanical toys, and packs of cards.

The minute Hank Steinberg stepped into the trailer, he wound up a mechanical metal roller coaster and started the cars zooming and diving.

"Now, what about Fenley Place—and why are you staring at my shoes?"

"It's a habit I've gotten into," Nancy said.

"They're Pacers. It's the hot shoe in California," Hank Steinberg said. "Have you got them here yet?"

"Yes," Nancy said. "I've been seeing them everywhere." Then to change the subject she asked, "Do you know about the things that have been happening over at the Teppingtons'?"

"Yes, I've heard, and I know everyone in the neighborhood thinks that *I'm* responsible. But I'm not. The crew thinks it's a publicity stunt, but that's crazy. We're not looking for any publicity. Anyway, the incidents at Fenley Place are making my people nervous, and they're making costly mistakes because of it."

Hank Steinberg watched the roller coaster for a few minutes in silence. Then he said, "I'm sure you've heard what's been happening on the set since we began filming in River Heights. It's almost as if someone's trying to sabotage my movie."

He walked back to Nancy and looked directly at her. "So, Ms. Drew," he said, "if you can solve the mystery, you'd be doing me a big favor."

"What are you filming tomorrow?" Nancy asked.

Hank Steinberg turned and pointed dramatically at Bess. Nancy relaxed a little. Bess's scene, with the red smoke, had already happened at Fenley Place. So there was nothing new to worry about, at least for a while.

"So, good night," Hank said. "See you in the movies."

Back in her car, Nancy looked up at the stars. "I don't think I can sleep tonight," she said. "My head's too full of this case." She turned to Bess. "Do you want to come over and spend the night? Maybe there'll be a good, old movie on TV."

"No thanks. I've got an eight o'clock call," Bess said. She had begun using a lot of movie expressions. "We actresses need our beauty rest."

"How about an old movie and popcorn?"

"Well . . . an actress needs her beauty rest *and* her popcorn," Bess answered.

* * *

Bess borrowed one of Nancy's nightgowns, and they sat on the couch in Nancy's living room, munching popcorn and watching a black-and-white horror movie on TV.

"Why are we watching this movie?" Bess asked with a yawn. "It's lousy."

"We're watching it because there's nothing else on," Nancy said.

Nancy and Bess stared at the screen. The movie was an old horror film called *Vampire Castle*. Even though they had tuned in late, it wasn't hard to follow the story.

A tall, pale man stood alone in the dimly lighted hall of a medieval castle. A beautiful young woman in a hooded cloak approached him. She folded down the hood to reveal her long, curly blond hair.

"Virginia," said the pale young man in a strange accent. "I told you to leave. You must leave immediately."

"I had to see you again," the actress replied. "I love you, Nigel."

"You can't. I am no longer Nigel. Now I am only a terrible monster," said the young man.

"Who are these people, anyway?" Bess moaned. "They can't act, and I bet they can't even scream."

"It's definitely *not* a Hank Steinberg film, that's for sure," Nancy agreed.

"Nigel, why are you staring at my neck?" asked the blond woman on the TV screen.

"Oh, no, Virginia," said Nigel, tearfully. "The evil curse has started already. I am becoming a vampire. You must leave and never come back."

Virginia wrapped her cloak tightly around her neck and turned slowly. Then the orchestra played louder as she walked out of the castle and closed the door. In a bright flash of light, Nigel turned into a bat and flew out the window.

The End. The movie credits started rolling by.

"Well, it's over," Nancy said. But Bess had fallen asleep with her hand in the popcorn bowl.

Nancy was too tired to get up and switch off the set, so she just sat there watching the credits. Suddenly a name jumped out of the screen. It was the name of the actress who had played the starring role of Virginia.

Nancy ran to the set to make sure she had read it correctly. No—there it was in big black-and-white letters. The actress who had played Virginia was Pamela *Teppington!*

10

Nancy Spots a Suspect

"Bess, wake up," Nancy said, shaking her sleeping friend.

Bess didn't know where she was for a minute.

"Pamela Teppington," Nancy said. "I just saw the name Pamela Teppington on TV."

"It's an okay name, Nancy," Bess said drowsily. "But I don't think I'm going to change my name for the movies—unless Hank thinks I should."

Bess slid down and stretched out on the couch. "Good night and thanks for thinking about me, Nancy," Bess said. She made a waving motion with her hand and fell back asleep.

Pamela Teppington—who was she? Nancy wondered. Was it just a coincidence? Or was she somehow related to the Teppingtons of Fenley Place?

Nancy grabbed a clock. It was two A.M. There was nothing to do but wait until morning. Then she'd spring the name on Alan Teppington and see how he reacted.

At eight A.M. Nancy hand-delivered Bess to Brandon Morris. He pointed them both to the makeup trailer parked at the end of Highland Avenue.

After Nancy had walked Bess over to the trailer, she said, "Now I've got to catch Alan Teppington before he goes to work."

"Wait a couple of minutes, okay, Nancy?" Bess begged. "Don't you want to see them put on my makeup?"

The trailer they were standing in was wall-to-wall lighted mirrors. There were also two sinks, plus a row of tall chairs facing the mirrors.

The door opened behind them and in walked a sleepy-eyed woman wearing a faded denim jumpsuit. She had elaborate green and blue eye shadow on and bright red lipstick. Nancy could tell right away that she was the makeup artist.

"Hi, I'm Adele," she said to Bess. "Are you a screamer, a bleeder, or a corpse?"

"Screamer," Bess said.

"Good," Adele said. "I don't think I could take another bleeder this early in the morning. It's gotten so bad I've even given up jelly doughnuts, you know what I mean?"

Bess nodded and sat down quickly in one of the chairs. "This will only take a minute, Nancy," Bess said.

"Actually, Nancy, it'll take a couple of hours," Adele said in a friendly voice, acting as though she had known Nancy for years. "First we have to wash her hair and style it. Then we have to start on the face."

Adele stuck a straw into a box of fruit juice and took a couple of sips. "Yeah," she said. "Screamers are easy. We keep the face kind of pale and darken the mouth a little so it shows up nice and big like a train tunnel. And we add lines around the eyes so they look enormous. But it takes two hours anyway because the hair stylist and I hate each other and we spend most of the time fighting and calling each other names."

"I really can't hang around for two hours," Nancy said, hopping off the chair she was sitting on. "I've got to go. Good luck, Bess. I'm sure you'll look gorgeous!"

Nancy ran out of the trailer and across the street to Fenley Place. The dark old house seemed to watch her with all the silent patience of a panther watching its prey.

Kate answered the door, wearing her pajamas.

"Hi, Kate," Nancy said. "Is your dad home?"

"He went to work. You just missed him."

"Oh, too bad." Nancy shook her head in disappointment. Then she noticed the dark circles under Kate's eyes. "Do you feel all right, Kate?"

"Amy had nightmares again. Nobody got much sleep," Kate said with a yawn. "We're making a welcome-home party for Boris. Want to help?"

"I can't, but give him a hug for me," Nancy said. "And tell your dad, I've got to talk to him. It's important."

Nancy headed back toward the makeup trailer. But as she approached it, she heard two angry voices arguing loudly. Adele and the hair stylist were at it already.

So instead of going in, Nancy veered toward the catering tent in the park. It was crowded and filled with delicious aromas. Nancy worked her way through the hungry movie cast and crew until she found George stationed by two juice dispensers and trays of warm miniature Danish.

"Hi, George, is it okay if I hang out here for a while? I want to *eavesdrop.*" Nancy whispered this last word.

But before George could answer, Pat Ellis, the owner of Elegant Eats walked up to them.

"George," said Pat Ellis, her dark eyes studying Nancy, "who's this? A friend?"

"This is my best friend, Nancy Drew."

Nancy opened her mouth to say hello, but Pat Ellis cut her off before she could get the word out.

"Are you busy?"

Nancy shook her head no.

"Well, would you like a job for a few hours? Three of my helpers didn't show up this morning. The pay is minimum wage plus all the Danish you can eat." Pat Ellis paused, as if to catch her breath. "What do you say?"

This might not be a bad place to observe every-one from, Nancy thought. She grinned and said to Pat, "George said the Danish are worth it. So why not!"

Pat put Nancy to work behind a steam table of poached eggs, in charge of either serving them bare or transforming them into Eggs Benedict.

As long as the food and the customers lasted, Nancy enjoyed the work. But as the morning wore on—and the food ran out—boredom set in. And she wasn't finding out anything new about Fenley Place.

How am I ever going to solve this mystery from here, Nancy thought to herself. Sipping a glass of orange juice, she looked around at the movie people talking and laughing.

Suddenly she almost choked. There was Spider Hutchings sitting under a tree talking to none other than Josh Petrie—the boy who had vandalized the Teppingtons' house!

"I thought he was in the army!" Nancy said out loud.

"Who?" the script girl standing nearby asked.

"Never mind."

Nancy quickly untied her apron. At the same time George came rushing up to her.

"Nancy, you'll never guess who's here," George said excitedly.

"I know. And I'm going to try to catch him," Nancy said, not taking her eyes off Josh Petrie for a second.

"Catch him? But he's here to see you!" George said.

"Huh?" Nancy said. "What are you talking about?" But she couldn't wait for George to explain. Josh was getting up and moving away. She zipped around the egg table and ran smack into the young man standing in front of her. It was Ned Nickerson, her boyfriend!

"Oooff! Hey—nice tackle! Maybe you should take up football," Ned said.

For a moment, Nancy was confused. She had been thinking about catching Josh Petrie, and here was Ned Nickerson. But Ned was supposed to be at his parents' summer house, at Cedar Lake. Nancy stared into his face as though he were the last person she expected to see, which he was.

"Ned?" she asked.

"Well, at least you haven't forgotten my name." Ned laughed. "For a second, I thought you were looking for someone else."

Nancy's eyes darted over to the tree where Josh and Spider had been sitting. But they were gone now. Two actresses in blood-stained clothes were sitting there instead, eating blueberry muffins.

"What are you doing here?" Nancy asked.

"Hank Steinberg doesn't come to River Heights every day," Ned said. "So I came to check out the action."

So far, the action had consisted of a puff of red smoke, a ghost in a window, a footprint in the dust, a drugged dog, and a terrorized family. Nancy figured it was more action than Ned had counted on.

"What's going on?" Ned asked. "I hear they're saying the movie is jinxed."

"Well, you know me," Nancy said. "I figure it's something a lot more real than a jinx or a rash of bad luck. But I haven't figured out *what*, yet."

"You will," Ned said. "You always do."

That was the great part about Ned Nickerson.

Nancy could always count on him to stick up for her.

"Did you see Josh Petrie a minute ago?" Nancy asked.

"He's not in town. He's in the army," Ned said.

"That's what I thought, too."

Just then Nancy heard a loud bell-buzzer—the signal that called the crew to work. It meant they were about to shoot a scene.

"Come on—we've got to go see Bess! She's got a part in the film," Nancy said.

"Screamer, bleeder, or corpse?" Ned said.

"That's what I like about you, Ned Nickerson. You catch on fast." Nancy grinned.

She looped her arm in Ned's and they hurried off toward the McCauley house. George had finished work until the next meal, so she went with them to watch Bess's scene.

On the sidewalk in front of the McCauley house stood Bess. Her face was made up, her hair was styled, and she was wearing a dress she couldn't afford even if she saved up all summer.

Hank Steinberg talked softly in her ear, giving her directions. He pointed to the McCauley house, but not at the chimney. From where Nancy stood, it looked like he was pointing at the walls.

Suddenly Nancy realized that Hank Steinberg had changed the script. He wasn't going to do the scene with the red smoke coming out of the chimney.

But what was he going to do instead?

"Quiet! This is a take!" one of the director's assistants called through a megaphone.

As Bess walked backward down the sidewalk, she focused her eyes on the front of the McCauley house.

Slowly, a small dark stream appeared on the wall. It trickled down from under the window ledge in a thin line. But soon it grew and spread out, forming large red blots. The house was bleeding, dripping with blood that poured slowly from under the roofline and the window sills, until nearly half of the front of the house was red.

Bess screamed her now-famous scream, and not even her friends knew whether she was faking it or not.

"Cut!" yelled Hank Steinberg.

Ned, standing next to Nancy, gave her a little poke with his elbow. "Hey, Nancy," he said. "Why are you looking away? You were never afraid of a little blood before? And this blood isn't even real!"

But Nancy wasn't looking *away* from the McCauley house. She was looking *at* Fenley Place, expecting at any minute to see blood begin to drip from its walls. It had to happen. It was in the script.

"Wash off the wall. I want to do it again," Hank Steinberg said.

During the next hour, they heard him give that order five more times. And they watched Bess scream five more times, each time sounding more terrified than the last.

And every time the red paint ran slowly down the

93

side of the McCauley house, Nancy's blood turned cold. She couldn't keep herself from looking behind her, hoping it wasn't happening at Fenley Place at the same time.

"This is great," Ned said. "And everything looks fine on the set. This movie doesn't look too jinxed to me."

But before the words were even out of Ned's mouth, a klieg light slipped off its scaffolding above the sidewalk. It came crashing down to the ground, hurtling toward Bess's head.

11

Alan Teppington's Story

It all happened too fast, before Nancy could shout out a warning to Bess.

As soon as Dallas saw the klieg light start to drop, he made a leaping dive from the sidelines straight at Bess. She didn't see him coming. And when he tackled her like a linebacker, her face had a look of genuine fear and pain.

A split second later the klieg light crashed to the sidewalk, shattering and sending glass fragments in all directions.

On the front lawn lay Bess and Dallas, both stunned and bruised by the impact of the collision.

Almost immediately they were surrounded by crew members and Hank Steinberg. Nancy, Ned, and George had a hard time getting through the crowd to Bess.

Dallas rolled on the grass, clutching at his left shoulder in pain. Stunt men like Spider Hutchings knew how to fall and roll. But a lighting man-turned-hero had to take his lumps.

"She's all right, Nancy," Ned said. "You can tell because she *sounds* all right."

Bess yelled in Hank Steinberg's face, "Did you do that just to scare me?" He was kneeling on the ground next to her, while crew members were helping Dallas to his feet. "You, you . . ." She stammered and searched for a word. "Jerk!"

"I realize you're upset—" Hank Steinberg said, but his voice wasn't rock-steady either.

"I'm not upset," Bess shouted. "I'm hysterical!"

"It was just an accident," said the director.

That word made Dallas furious.

"Accident? There's been one too many accidents around here, Mr. Steinberg," he said. "If there's another one, or if anything else strange happens to that house across the street, I quit!"

Hank Steinberg saw a hot situation getting hotter and knew that he'd better act quickly to cool it down.

"Take thirty minutes," he called to everybody. He thanked Bess for her scream and then personally asked the crowd of onlookers to go away and come back another time.

Nancy and her friends rushed over to make sure Bess was all right. She was a little shaky and bruised but otherwise unhurt.

"Well what do you want to do now?" Ned said in a disappointed voice. "Now that Hollywood Heights has asked us to please leave."

"I'll tell you what I'd *like* to do," Nancy replied. "Find Josh Petrie! I'm positive I saw him with Spider Hutchings this morning."

"I say we forget about *Terror Weekend* and Fenley Place, at least for today," George said, "and go for a swim!"

Bess agreed. She asked them to wait while she changed her clothes and took off her makeup. Then the four friends made quick steps to pick up their beach gear and headed for a nearby lake.

By the end of the day, they were all a little sunburned but relaxed and happy. Even Nancy agreed that she was glad to forget about the Teppingtons for a while.

But at the pizza restaurant that night, the four of them found themselves once again thinking about the events over on Highland Avenue.

"You know, if I lived on that street, I think I'd be spooked," George said. "And I don't believe in ghosts."

"Can you imagine how the Teppingtons feel?" said Bess. "I mean, they're just sitting around waiting for something awful to happen."

Nancy kept time with her thoughts, tapping one fingernail on the table until Ned put his hand over hers.

"What are you thinking about?" he asked.

"The script," Nancy said. "Why did Hank Steinberg change the script?"

"Nancy!" George said. "Look who's here!"

"Who? Where?"

"At the corner table with those creeps from the bowling alley."

Nancy followed George's eyes and saw Josh Petrie. He was just getting comfortable at a small table with some very rough-looking friends.

"This time he's not getting away," Nancy said, standing up. She marched over to Josh's table.

"How's it going, girl detective," Josh said, briefly glancing up at Nancy. Even when there wasn't a sneer on his face, there was one in his voice.

"Hi, Josh," Nancy said. " I thought you were in the army."

"And I thought you were sitting over there," he fired back. Josh Petrie did everything quickly. You could tell he never thought about what he said before he spoke.

"Seriously, I heard you enlisted," Nancy said, trying to look into Josh's brown eyes.

He held the plastic laminated menu in both hands and drummed the edge of the table with it. "It didn't go," he said. "I got kicked out. Dishonorable discharge, stealing. Have I made your night? Now, bug off!"

Josh pushed his chair back to get away from Nancy, but she didn't leave.

"I said, get out of here!" Josh was almost shouting.

"Listen, Josh, a friend of mine almost got killed on the movie set today," she said. "And weird things keep going on at Fenley Place. What do you know about it?"

"I don't know what you're talking about," he said calmly. "I haven't been near there."

"Let me see your shoes, Josh."

"Take a hike," he said.

Nancy turned to leave, but Josh was leaning back in his chair, and she couldn't get through.

"Excuse me," she said to the man sitting at the table behind Josh. The man scooted his chair sideways and accidentally bumped into Josh. Josh fell backward and landed on the floor with his feet stuck straight up in the air, showing Nancy a brand new pair of Pacer track shoes.

"You'd better be telling me the truth, Josh," Nancy said, walking away.

"Listen," Josh yelled after her. "Anytime the Teppingtons get dumped on is okay with me. Got that?"

After that, Nancy wasn't too hungry. So she and Ned said good night to Bess and George and headed toward Ned's car. The night was strangely quiet. Only a handful of crickets were chirping in front lawns when usually there were choirs.

"Josh Petrie is never happy unless he's causing trouble," Ned said.

"That's what I'm afraid of," Nancy said. But she tried to put Josh Petrie out of her mind for the moment. "What time is it?" she asked Ned. "I've still got to catch Alan Teppington and ask him a question."

"Almost midnight. I've got to get back to my parents' place."

"You're not staying?" Nancy asked Ned.

"I can't," he answered. "We have guests coming tomorrow. I just came to check out the movie stars, watch Bess almost get mashed by a klieg light, and catch you picking a fight with Josh Petrie. Who could ask for more?"

"Very funny," Nancy said. "So where's your car?"

Nancy and Ned turned the corner toward the city lot where Ned had parked earlier that day.

Because Ned had a long trip ahead of him, Nancy insisted that he drop her off at the corner of Highland Avenue. She said goodbye and promised to write to him soon—as soon as she solved the case.

"Good luck," he called as he pulled away from the curb.

A nearby church tower clanged twelve as she walked down the street toward the Teppingtons' house.

Was she too late? Was it happening right then to the walls of Fenley Place? Would the house be covered in blood as the McCauley house had been?

When Nancy saw Fenley Place, she sighed with relief. The large mustard-colored house shone gold in the moonlight. There was no sign of blood.

A light in the den, visible from the street, lured her on.

Alan Teppington, in his baggy, striped robe, answered the door and led Nancy into the den, where he and Sara were playing cards.

The Teppingtons wanted to know how Bess was. Sara had seen the klieg light fall.

"Then you must have seen the McCauley house

100

dripping with red paint." Nancy made sure to use the word *paint* instead of *blood*.

The Teppingtons nodded.

"I never liked the color of this house anyway," Sara joked half-heartedly.

"Mr. Teppington," Nancy said, coming to the point of her visit. "I watched the late show last night. The movie was called *Vampire Castle*."

Alan Teppington's whole expression changed. He looked as though he didn't want to talk about the subject Nancy had brought up. He scooped up the cards and started laying out a hand of solitaire on the table.

"Who is Pamela Teppington? Is she a relative of yours?"

Boris, asleep on the floor, gave a low growl that stuck in his throat. His legs twitched.

"Pamela Teppington is my ex-wife," said Alan Teppington.

Above their heads, Fenley Place creaked and sagged. Nancy's back straightened.

"It was twenty years ago. I was very young. We weren't married for very long," Alan said. "Six months."

Snap! went the cards as he continued to deal the solitaire hand.

"Pamela and I met in high school and got married right after graduation. Then we went out to Hollywood together. But I think she just married me to get out of River Heights. She loved the idea of being a big star more than anything else. After she did *Vampire Castle*, I never saw her again."

101

He swept his arm across the table and the cards flew to the floor.

"So you can see why I despise show business people." He stood up to go to bed.

Was there a coincidence, Nancy asked herself? Alan's ex-wife was in a horror movie, and now there was a horror movie being filmed across the street. Was Pamela Teppington somehow connected with Hank Steinberg's production?

"Mr. Teppington, where is your ex-wife now?" Nancy asked.

"I told you. I haven't seen her in twenty years!" he exploded.

The den door slammed against the wall as he opened it and stomped out.

"I'm sorry," Nancy said to Sara. "I didn't mean to—"

"It's all right. He always acts like that when Pamela's name is mentioned," Sara said. "Fortunately, it doesn't get mentioned very often."

"Mrs. Teppington," Nancy began.

"Sara," the woman reminded her.

"Right. Sara. If I'm going to find out who's been doing these terrible things to you, I've got to be here when it happens. Do you mind if I sleep here tonight?"

"Are you expecting something to happen, Nancy?" Sara asked anxiously.

"I don't know," Nancy said. "But I think I should be here, just in case."

* * *

Later, sitting on the living room couch alone, Nancy listened to the house.

Click, click, click.

Nancy caught her breath. It was Boris's paw nails on the wood floor. He jumped up on the couch and fell asleep. Nancy fought him for foot room the whole night. But finally she, too, fell asleep.

At six A.M. something woke Nancy up. She sat up on the couch and saw the first pink splashes of sunlight in the morning sky.

But what had awakened her? Was it a sound on the front porch?

She slipped on her shoes and walked softly to the front door. As she stepped out onto the porch, Nancy could see the answer.

There was red everywhere—streaks of dark red blood.

The whole front of the house was covered with it.

12

Alone in the House

Right away, Nancy could tell that it was paint and not real blood. Just the same, it looked awful. The color was perfect—it looked exactly like blood. Nancy touched the paint and found that it was dry.

Just then Boris charged out of the house, barking and snapping fiercely.

"Quiet! It's me!" Nancy said in exasperation.

The dog finally stopped barking and lay down glumly on the porch, blocking the steps. He put his chin on his front paws.

"What's going on?" Alan Teppington asked, stepping out onto the porch in his robe. "We heard Boris barking."

Sara was only a few steps behind her husband. They were both looking at the dog, but then they turned and saw what had been done to their house.

"That's it!" Alan Teppington said. He flew back inside like a man with a definite plan of action.

"When did this happen?" Sara asked Nancy.

Nancy wished she had something better to say.

"I was asleep. I didn't hear anything. I just found it," she said.

"I'll go call the police. We're practically on a first-name basis," Sara said.

When a squad car pulled into the driveway of Fenley Place, two officers and a sergeant got out slowly. The sergeant stared at the house, then ordered his men to get to work. Alan Teppington came back out of the house dressed.

"Sergeant Velez, folks," the officer in charge said, introducing himself. "We're going to check the porch and search around the house. It won't take long."

"Make it fast. We're leaving as soon as you're done," Alan told the police.

The sergeant wiped his forehead. "It's going to be a hot one today," he said. "Anyone hear anything last night?"

"We were all asleep," Sara said.

"Is the dog deaf?" Sergeant Velez asked.

"No, just useless," Alan snapped.

"Sound sleeper," Nancy said. It was the kindest thing she could say about her couchmate.

The noise of the investigation woke the Teppington children, and they appeared on the porch. Kate took one look at the house and then ran down the porch steps onto the lawn.

"Daddy, carry me," Amy cried, rubbing her sleepy eyes. "I don't want the blood to get on me."

"It's paint, Sergeant," one of the officers called.

"Well," the sergeant said to Sara and Alan, "if

105

you get yourself a new paint job, you'll never know it was there."

Apparently, he thought he was giving the Teppingtons some good news.

"Have you seen the McCauley house?" Alan said.

"Sure," replied the sergeant. "That's where they're making the movie."

"The McCauleys are making a fortune letting Hank Steinberg wreck their house. And the city is getting a fat fee, too, for putting up with those phonies. But whatever happens to my house, happens for free! Except I've got to pay to replace my windows and for a new paint job. Is that right?"

Nancy could tell that the sergeant didn't have an answer or an idea about how to help the Teppingtons.

"What happens there, happens here, huh," Velez said thoughtfully. "Well, what are they going to do next over there?"

Since no one knew, he sent one of his officers across the street to find out. In the meantime, he took out his handkerchief and wiped his forehead again.

Ten minutes later, the officer returned from the McCauley house. "They're burning the house down tomorrow, sir," she reported.

"They're doing *what?*" Sergeant Velez was aghast.

"That's what someone said," the officer answered with a shrug.

The sergeant loosened his tie and his collar button, and spoke to the Teppingtons. "Okay, folks, right now we don't have a single clue as to who did this," he said.

"Or *what* did this," Alan Teppington said, looking bitterly at his house.

"They only pay me to find the *whos*, Mr. Teppington," the sergeant said. "I'm sorry. We'll be in touch."

Then Sergeant Velez and his officers got into their squad car and pulled away.

"I don't believe those guys," Alan said, slapping his hand on the red wall.

"Alan," Sara said calmly. "I don't think we should leave."

"Why not?" Alan asked. "You want to stick around for the barbecue? I know you *love* toasted marshmallows."

"All right, all right!" Sara said. "If it'll stop your sarcasm, I'll go. Maybe we can finally get some rest."

"Great!" Alan looked truly happy for the first time since Nancy met him. "Now, girls, pack up your toys quickly. We're going to stay in a motel for a few days. Hurry up, Kate."

"No," Nancy said. "Take your time."

The Teppingtons looked at her, waiting for an explanation.

"I mean, I think going away is a good idea," Nancy said. "But could you pack up the car slowly, so that everyone can see that you're leaving?"

"What are you planning to do?"

"If you don't mind, I'm going to stay in your house," Nancy said.

"Out of the question," Alan answered quickly. "It's too dangerous."

"It's the only way I can find out who's doing this," Nancy said firmly. "If it *is* Josh Petrie or someone on the movie crew, he may not be so careful if he thinks you're gone."

"I don't know," Alan said doubtfully.

"You can tell me I can't do it, but you can't tell me it's not the best plan," Nancy said.

In the end, the Teppingtons loaded their station wagon slowly, locked their front door, and drove away. Nancy pretended to leave, too. She waved goodbye and walked all the way to the end of Highland Avenue. After about fifteen minutes, she walked back to Fenley Place quickly, glancing around to make sure she wasn't noticed. She was relieved to find that no one in front of the McCauley house was looking her way. She crept quietly through the front gate and around to the back of the house. Then she let herself into the back door using Alan's key.

The first thing Nancy did was to look up inside the chimney again. Yes, the lump was still there. Sooner or later, Nancy decided, she was going to find out what it was.

But something made her stop looking up the chimney and look behind her instead. She felt as though someone were watching her. No, that couldn't be—not in an empty house.

Suddenly Nancy realized that she had been up for hours without eating. She was starving.

She went down the hall to the kitchen, stopping at the stairs leading to the second floor. It was dark and quiet up there.

Nancy kept walking to the kitchen.

There's no bigger mystery than someone else's kitchen, Nancy thought, remembering one of Hannah Gruen's old sayings.

The refrigerator was almost empty. There were only a couple of eggs and some butter. In the bag of bread only heels were left.

Nancy pulled open a cabinet drawer. It was filled with sharpened knives and shish-kabob skewers. She closed it quickly and tried another drawer, but it was locked.

Finally, she left the kitchen, munching a handful of sweet dry cereal.

In the hall, Nancy stopped at the steps to the second floor again. An unpleasant odor wafted down to her on a thin, hot breeze. She decided to go upstairs.

Floorboards creaked under her feet as she crept up the steps. She wondered why she was trying to sneak upstairs when there was nobody else in the house.

On a carved wooden table on the second-floor landing, cut flowers had been left too long in a vase. The water was murky and the smell of rotting flowers was quite strong.

They had to be thrown out. She was just about to carry the vase away, when she heard noises downstairs. Someone was walking back and forth on the porch. Nancy listened carefully. The footsteps stopped, then started again. Whoever it was was probably looking in the windows, she reasoned.

Nancy hurried downstairs and yanked open the door to give her guest a little surprise.

She and her guest were both surprised. Chris Hitchcock, the boy she had met on the day of Bess's audition, stood on the porch with his arms around a heavy basket of Hawaiian fruit and flower leis.

"Hey, I didn't even ring the bell. You must be psychic," Chris said, laughing. "Peace offering from Hank Steinberg. Tell 'em I'm here. I can't wait to see Alan Teppington's face."

"You'll have to wait. They're gone," Nancy said.

"They are? When will they be back?"

Nancy shrugged. Chris set the basket down on the porch and knelt to tie the shoelace of one of his Pacer track shoes.

"Nice shoes," Nancy said.

"They're *in* this week. Everybody got them before we left L.A.," Chris said. "So what are you doing here—snooping around or guarding the house?"

"A little bit of both," Nancy said, then she changed the subject quickly. "Tell me something: Why does Hank Steinberg want to make peace?"

"I don't know," Chris said. "I guess just in case there's any bad *blood* between them." Chris laughed and then stopped. "I guess that wasn't so funny, was it?"

Nancy had to agree.

"Okay, here's the truth: Hank's feeling guilty about all the stuff going on over here," Chris said, more seriously. "I mean, Hank is so into horror movies that he actually thinks this house might be haunted. He thinks *he* brought the bad luck to River Heights."

"I'm not so sure he's wrong," Nancy said.

"Well, Hank can't blame this basket of fruit on the supernatural," Chris said. "This is his own mistake."

"What do you mean? It looks delicious," Nancy said.

"Hank doesn't know that Alan Teppington is allergic to pineapple," Chris said. "He ate some when I was here, scouting for a location. One bite and he started wheezing like crazy. Do you think he's going to suddenly love movie people after he sees this? No way!"

As Nancy and Chris talked, another voice joined their conversation. It was a thin voice, interrupted by static and it came from Chris's walkie-talkie.

"They're calling me. Well, I've got to run," Chris said, taking the porch steps in one jump. "Enjoy the fruit."

After he left, the sun moved slowly overhead, raising the temperature in the house. Nancy went back upstairs to throw out the dead flowers and wash the vase.

Standing by the table on the landing, she became aware of a flapping sound in the house. It would beat out a message, then fall quiet and start again.

Curtains blowing in the wind, Nancy thought, but there was no wind blowing through Fenley Place. She was keeping the windows closed, so it would look like the Teppingtons were really gone.

The sound seemed to be coming from the third-floor attic. As Nancy climbed the stairs to the third floor, the noise definitely got louder.

She opened the door and walked slowly into the attic. For a moment, all was still.

Then suddenly a bird darted toward her face. She ducked and it flew out the front window, the way it had come in.

How did that window get open? Nancy wondered.

She pushed boxes out of her way to get through to the window so she could close it.

And that's when she saw the silver blue tack hammered into the molding. Dangling from it was a thin, clear plastic line, like fishing line. She stretched out the plastic line and found that it reached to a tack on the other side of the window.

As Nancy removed and coiled the line, something crashed on the roof over her head. She held her breath and waited.

Next she heard steps, quick steps. They came from above her on the roof!

Moving quietly on tiptoe until she reached the stairs, Nancy listened to the footsteps still tapping above her. She ran downstairs as fast as she could run, her heart beating quickly.

In seconds she was out of the house and on the

front lawn. Squinting into the sun, she saw a hunched figure darting across the roof.

"Hey!" Nancy shouted. "What are you doing up there?"

But the figure disappeared around the chimney before Nancy could see who it was.

13

Special Effects

Nancy ran around to the side of the house just in time to see the figure of a young man climbing over a dormer window which stuck up in the roof.

"Hey!" she yelled. "You've got to come down sometime!"

"Catch me!" the guy called back.

She ran back to the front yard again.

"Chris?" Now Nancy recognized him and his white jeans as he stepped into view. "What are you doing up on the roof?"

"What are you doing down there?" he answered playfully.

"Watching you break your neck. Now get down!"

Out of the corner of her eye, Nancy saw that she wasn't alone on the front lawn of Fenley Place. Standing nearby was a girl who was about four inches taller than Nancy, which made her almost six feet tall. She was looking up at the roof, too. She had dark curls that fell down the back of her *Terror Weekend* T-shirt.

"Hi, I'm Jane," the tall girl said.

114

"I'm Nancy. Maybe we can ride to his funeral together."

"Don't worry about Chris," Jane said. "You should have seen him climb up there—it's like he was born to be a stunt man. But he's got bigger dreams than that."

"What kind of dreams?" Nancy asked.

"He wants to be a director. Like his idol, Alfred Hitchcock," Jane answered. Then she added, "Hitchcock's not Chris's real name, you know."

"I know." Nancy looked back toward the roof. "Come down, will you?" she shouted.

"I can't," Chris yelled back. "I'm looking for something I lost."

While she watched and waited, Nancy studied the plastic wire she had found in the attic. Then she placed it back in her pocket.

"Got it!" Chris shouted waving a bright red frisbee in his hand. He tossed it down to Nancy and Jane. Then without thinking twice, Chris leapt onto the limb of a tree that was overhanging the roof. He hoisted himself up onto the limb and, straddling it, scooted to the tree trunk. Then he climbed down.

"You look like you've done that before," Nancy said, when Chris joined them.

"My uncle's got an apple farm. I've been climbing his trees for years," Chris said. "I can't let a little roof stop me from finishing my game."

Jane laughed. "I swear you threw it up there on purpose," she said. "I mean, I'm tall, but I'm not *that* tall, right?"

Chris pretended to be offended. "Well, if you're going to make fun of me," he said, "I'll just take my toy and go home."

He walked off in the direction of the McCauley house. Nancy thought he was just kidding and that he'd come back, but he didn't.

"He's a crazy guy," Jane said, laughing again.

"Yes, he is," Nancy said, shaking her head.

"He loves movies," Jane said. "He loves to make them, and he loves to talk about them. I heard his mother's a movie star, but who knows? Chris would probably make up that rumor himself."

"Jane, who would I see if I needed more of this stuff?" Nancy asked. She held out the thin plastic wire from the attic.

"Special effects," Jane said. "Come on. I'll show you."

Jane took Nancy to the special effects trailer which was part laboratory and part storage vault.

The man who ran the place looked like a modern-day mad scientist. He wore a gray sweatshirt and he had a scruffy brown beard. His hair seemed to have been given a life-time dose of static electricity.

"Bo Aronson, this is Nancy. See you later," Jane said.

"Just a sec," he said. He was working on a severed hand at his workbench. Finally he looked up and asked the inevitable question.

"Screamer, bleeder, or corpse?"

"Visitor," Nancy said.

"Great. Stand right there. Don't move," Bo Aron-

116

son slid his chair over to Nancy, carrying the fake hand. "Hold it near your neck."

Nancy examined the hand first. It was heavy, and seemed to be metal inside and rubber and plastic outside. Then she did as he had asked.

Bo picked up a remote control unit, the kind that came with battery-powered toys.

"Got an itch?" Bo said, moving one of the control sticks.

A finger on the hand began to scratch Nancy's neck.

"That's the worst thing I've ever felt in my life," Nancy said, with a shudder.

Bo moved another control, and the hand opened and grabbed Nancy's throat. She pulled it away.

"After the movie I may put it on the market. I'll call it the Babysitter's Friend, guaranteed to quiet noisy kids. What do you think?"

"I think you ought to sell gloves to go with it," Nancy said.

"You've got a good head on your shoulders," Bo said. "That's a shame because I've got a dozen of them in a cabinet just waiting around." They both laughed.

Nancy changed the subject. "What's this wire?" she asked, tossing Bo the plastic wire she was carrying.

"This is monofilament wire, and it's everything to a special effects man," he said. "It's so superthin and transparent, it's practically invisible."

Bo showed her how he might use the wire in a movie. "I can send a knife zipping straight into your heart. I can make a dozen cobras stand at attention ready to strike. I can make furniture fly around the room or bats flap outside your window."

"And you can't see the wire in the movie?" Nancy said.

"Not if the lighting is right," Bo said. "In one movie, I attached a ghost to the tail of a horse with monofilament. When the horse ran, the ghost took off like a kite. It looked like the ghost was chasing the horse everywhere. And that was during the daytime. A much trickier shot."

He rummaged over a desktop crowded with blueprints and plastic dead rats, tubes of paint, and tools. Finally he held up something in a white plastic bag. "Do you know what this is?" he asked holding it above his head.

Nancy was afraid to ask.

"It's ham and cheese on whole wheat. It's my lunch!" Bo laughed. "Want to share it? We can wash it down with this." Bo held up a bottle with a red liquid.

"Blood?" gasped Nancy.

"Cherry soda," Bo said. "But the blood is drinkable too. It's corn syrup with red dye." He flipped open a cabinet that contained twelve bottles of fake blood.

Bo took a big chomp out of his sandwich, and Nancy started to leave. But then she noticed something with an unusual shape on his table. It was covered over by a large cloth. Bo could tell she wanted to know what it was.

"Go ahead," he said. "Take a look."

Nancy moved toward the table and lifted the cloth. Underneath was a wooden model that looked like the McCauley house. It was perfect in every detail.

"Say goodbye to the McCauley house," Bo said. "We're burning her next week."

"How can you burn the McCauley house?" Nancy asked incredulously.

"We can't," Bo said. "That's why we're going to burn this model in my special effects studio back in L.A. I've been working on this all week. In fact, when I'm done I'll have built the whole neighborhood."

"Are you sure they're not going to burn any part of the real McCauley house?" Nancy asked anxiously.

"I didn't say that," Bo replied. "We'll make some flames shoot out of the windows. And Hank insists that we set a few fires on the roof. But we'll use a fireproof pad under the fire, don't worry."

"When?" Nancy asked.

"Tomorrow," Bo said.

Well, Nancy thought, at least that gives me one more day.

"I'll show you something else," he said, stuffing the rest of the sandwich into his mouth. He opened a cabinet and banged around the shelves looking for something. "Can't find it," he said. "This film has been the worst."

"What do you mean?"

"Never mind," Bo answered.

Nancy guessed what he was talking about. As

George had said, things were disappearing from the set.

"Bo, have you heard about what's been going on at Fenley Place?" Nancy asked.

"Sure," he said. "The Double Horror of Fenley Place, I call it. Everything that we shoot happens over there for real. It would make a great movie."

"Well, I've been trying to solve the mystery," Nancy said, dropping her voice. "In fact, I found that piece of monofilament wire in the attic at Fenley Place. If you can help me, maybe I can help you find out who's been stealing from you."

"A detective, huh?" Bo asked with a smile.

Nancy had heard this kind of mocking reaction before, and she always ignored it.

"What kinds of things have been stolen, Bo?"

"I'm used to losing some blood capsules here, a trick knife there," he answered. "I can understand people taking the fun stuff for souvenirs and all. But this time you'd think someone was planning to rob a bank or something. I lost some explosives and a remote detonator—small stuff, but enough to liven up somebody's Fourth of July."

Nancy kept quiet because she wanted to hear more.

Bo opened a drawer and handed Nancy a medicine bottle full of capsules. "Maybe you'd be interested in this," he said.

"What does it do?" Nancy asked.

"It's not a special effect," Bo said, shaking his head. "It's just a bottle of pills. I found it on the floor in here one morning when I came to work. Later that day I noticed some things were missing."

Now that she realized the thief may have dropped the bottle, Nancy looked at it more carefully. The medicine was ordinary looking. It was the prescription label, glued around the outside of the bottle, that was strange.

The top half of the label—the half with the name of the patient—had been deliberately torn off. Only the medication instructions remained: "Take one tablet every six hours for allergy and asthma."

"Now, why would someone tear his name off his prescription bottle?" asked Bo.

"Yes," Nancy agreed. "Especially since he couldn't know he was going to drop it in your trailer." Nancy thought for a moment.

"Do you know anyone on the movie crew who has asthma or a serious allergy?"

Bo shook his head. "This *is* a pretty good mystery," he said.

"Well," Nancy said. "I just found out today about someone who is very allergic to pineapple." She rolled the bottle of pills in her hand.

"Who is it?" Bo asked.

"Alan Teppington," she answered. "But what I can't figure out is this: why would a man want to vandalize his own house and terrorize his own family?"

14

Prescription for Terror

The bottle of pills made Nancy think about Alan Teppington in a new light. Maybe he wasn't just a victim of the double horror of Fenley Place as he said. Maybe this man with his explosive temper hated Fenley Place so much that he created the terror. But why?

"It's hard to believe," Nancy said out loud.

"Thanks," Bo Aronson said. He assumed her comment was a compliment for the half-dozen mechanical cockroaches he had just set off on the floor.

Nancy, who had been staring off into space, looked down at the floor for the first time and screamed.

"You should have auditioned," Bo said.

Nancy calmed down quickly as soon as she realized the roaches weren't real. "I've got to find out whose pills these are," she said, as she stepped carefully to the door.

"Yeah, sure," Bo said, still watching his roaches scurry around. "Listen, would you like to take a couple of these to remember me by?"

Nancy looked at the bugs on the floor and shook her head no.

"Not those guys," Bo said. "These." He handed her two small red plastic capsules. "Blood capsules. Squash 'em in your hand, crush 'em with your teeth. Everybody goes crazy over these."

"Thanks," Nancy said, although she didn't know how she could possibly use them.

After leaving Bo's trailer, Nancy's first stop was the Elegant Eats tent. Nancy wanted to find out if someone in the movie company had a food allergy —an allergy that required medication. And maybe, she hoped, George would be the person who could tell her.

The afternoon sun was hot, and the gold chain Nancy wore around her neck clung to her skin. For a moment, as she walked, it felt like the mechanical hand on her throat.

The catering tent, as usual, was crowded, but George was nowhere to be seen.

So Nancy stopped the first person she saw wearing one of Pat Ellis's striped aprons. The girl used one hand to carry a large tray of dirty dishes and her other hand to straight-arm people out of her way.

"Do you know where George Fayne is?" Nancy asked.

"Who's he?" asked the girl who was chewing on what seemed like ten sticks of gum.

"George is a *she*," Nancy said.

The girl looked at Nancy and shouldn't have. It caused the tray of dishes she was carrying to tilt, slip, and then fall all over two men unlucky enough to be sitting nearby.

Nancy had looked away before the crash, and when she turned back she saw that the dishes had fallen on Deck Burroughs. Spider Hutchings was sitting by Deck, but the dishes missed him completely.

"Hey, you're my stunt man," Deck said to Spider while he brushed food off his T-shirt. "Stuff like this is supposed to happen to you."

Spider was laughing too hard to answer.

"It's all *her* fault," the girl said, pointing at Nancy.

Deck and Spider stood up, looking at Nancy, and she blushed. Deck Burroughs's clothes and black hair were a mess, but his eyes were still a bright, electric blue.

"I'm really sorry," Nancy said. "Can I get you something? A paper towel or some napkins?" She grabbed a handful of napkins from a nearby table and handed them to Deck.

"She probably just wanted to look at your shoes," Spider said. "She's got a thing about shoes."

Nancy and Deck both looked down at Deck's feet at the same time. He was barefoot, except for some scraps of fruit salad.

"I don't know what to say," Nancy said, smiling. "I don't usually dump food on people."

"Well, I'm not used to being dumped on," Deck grinned. "Why don't we just say it's been an experience."

"Good idea," Nancy said.

He held out his hand to shake hers. "Deck Burroughs," he said, as if she didn't know.

"Nancy Drew," said Nancy, trying to ignore the potato salad in his palm as she shook his hand.

"You'll have to excuse me," Deck said very formally to Nancy, Spider, and the gum-chewing catering helper. "I think I'm beginning to attract flies."

He left the park quickly.

Nancy made a quick retreat into the kitchen area, where she found George. Her friend was cleaning and cutting mountains of vegetables and tossing them into a large caldron of broth on a stove behind her. When she saw Nancy, she stopped working for a minute and picked up a carrot stick.

"What's up, doc?" George asked, chomping into the carrot.

"I just accidentally made someone dump a tray of dirty dishes on Deck Burroughs," Nancy said. Her face grew warm again at the memory.

George giggled. "Well, just tell him he's going to have to wait for the second course. The soup's not ready yet."

"Ha, ha," Nancy said dryly. "He was very understanding about it—understanding and very *sticky.*"

"I'll bet," George said. "He's really nice, though, did you notice? I mean, he hangs around with the crew members and eats with Spider every day. Not like some of the other actors, who complain about the food, even though it's delicious. Some of these guys are real pills."

"Pills! George, that's exactly why I was looking for you!" Nancy said. She held up the medicine bottle between her thumb and index finger.

"What's that?" asked George.

"A real clue, if I can find the owner of this bottle," Nancy said excitedly. "Any of the movie cast or crew ever talk about having asthma or a food allergy?"

"Come on, Nancy. With so many people screaming, choking, and just acting strange in this movie, someone with asthma would have a tough time getting noticed," George said.

"I guess," Nancy said.

But suddenly George's face lit up and she pointed a finger at Nancy. "Spider Hutchings," she said.

"What about him?" Nancy asked.

"He wouldn't take a piece of date nut bread from me," George said. "I said, 'Go ahead. Take it. You can always work off the calories by jumping out of a tree, or something.' But he said no. He's allergic to nuts."

"Spider Hutchings!" Nancy cried. "He's right outside."

Nancy ran back into the park which was just as crowded as it was before.

Where was he?

Nancy stopped the first person she saw, which

happened to be the gum-chewing waitress. This time, she wasn't carrying any dishes. "Did you see Spider Hutchings?" asked Nancy.

"Is that a *he* or a *she?*" asked the girl, as she snapped her gum.

Nancy rolled her eyes. "Never mind," she said, rushing out toward the street.

She looked up and down both sides of Highland Avenue, but she couldn't see Spider anywhere.

Maybe he's shooting a stunt, she thought, and started walking to the McCauley house.

"Is Spider Hutchings here?" Nancy asked the security man stationed at the front door of the McCauley house.

"Not yet, but he will be. He's got to jump through a window this afternoon."

"Great! Can I wait for him? It's very important," Nancy said.

"You'll have to ask the assistant director about that, miss," said the guard.

The assistant director said Nancy could wait if she kept out of everyone's way. So Nancy tried to melt into the wallpaper in the McCauley house's lavish living room.

The crew was working some of Bo Aronson's magic that afternoon. At the director's command, a button was pushed, a pulley turned, and the living room couch lifted off the ground. Next, a reading chair, a table, and a TV taxied and then launched themselves around the room.

"Monofilament wire," Nancy said to herself.

Just when all of the furniture was in the air, the phone on the writing desk started ringing and ringing, even though its handset was off the hook. It was all just as Nancy had read in the shooting script.

The crew kept trying different effects. Nancy was starting to feel impatient. When would Spider show up?

Then she glanced out the picture window and saw Spider Hutchings doing push-ups on the lawn. She rushed out before he could get away again.

"Spider, I've got to talk to you," Nancy asked.

"Give me a chance to put on a raincoat first," Spider teased.

"No dirty dishes this time," Nancy said. "Just a present for you."

"What's this?" Spider asked, looking at the medicine bottle Nancy had given him.

"I found your medicine," Nancy said.

"Someone's pulling your leg," Spider said. "I don't pollute my body with medicines."

"Aren't you allergic to nuts?"

"Yeah, nuts, bananas, and eggs," Spider said. "But I don't take pills for that; I just don't eat them. Listen, I hate to cut this short, but right now I've got to go smash some glass."

Nancy took back the pills and walked with him toward the McCauley house. "Are you and Josh Petrie close friends?" she asked.

"No," Spider answered. "We just met a couple of days ago. You know old Josh doesn't have too many

128

good things to say about you. He says you're always trying to get him into trouble."

"He usually doesn't need anybody's help to do *that*," Nancy said. "But he does have a grudge against the Teppingtons, the people who own Fenley Place."

"You're back to that again," Spider said, brushing his red hair back with his hand.

"I don't quit. Did he tell you anything about what he did to the Teppingtons last year?" Nancy asked.

"All he told me was how he wanted to be a stunt man, and he asked if I could get him started," Spider said. "I said it's as good a way as any to get his neck broken. He seems like an all-right guy, so I've been showing him the ropes—excuse the pun. That's all."

Spider gave Nancy a smile and a little salutelike wave and walked into the house, calling out, "Window remover's here!"

As Nancy turned away, someone on the front lawn shouted through a megaphone: "Is there a Nancy Drew here?"

"That's me!" Nancy called.

"There's someone outside the barricades who wants to see you," the megaphone answered.

"Screamer, bleeder, or corpse?" Nancy asked with a laugh.

"Looks to me like a little of each," the voice said.

Nancy hurried to the end of the block and found Hannah Gruen waiting for her. Hannah's usually smooth, calm face was lined with tension and, worse than that, fear.

"What is it?" Nancy asked. "Is something wrong with Dad?"

"No," Hannah said. "But you've got to come home right away. The horror has moved to our house!"

15

A Major Clue

Hannah Gruen wiped her forehead with a linen handkerchief she had tucked in the sleeve of her blouse. "I was only gone an hour doing some shopping," Hannah said. "When I came home, the house looked like it was dumped upside down."

"Oh, no!" Nancy said. "We'd better hurry. Where's your car?"

"I took a cab," Hannah answered. "I was just too shaken up to drive."

Nancy and Hannah hurried to Nancy's blue sportscar and started driving back to the Drew house.

"It's the strangest thing I've ever seen," Hannah continued. "The furniture is everywhere it's not supposed to be. Dining chairs in the hall, the couch on the other side of the room, tables moved every which way. It's as though they waited till I was gone and then flew around the room."

Nancy tried to be calm. But she had just seen what Hannah had described. What she didn't understand was how furniture could fly without mon-ofilament wire.

"But that's not all of it," Hannah said. "I wasn't in the house five minutes, when the phone began to ring. And it wouldn't stop—"

Nancy knew the ending to Hannah's sentence and she finished it for her. "Not even when you picked up the receiver," Nancy said.

Hannah's face registered additional surprise. "How could you possibly know that?" Hannah asked.

"Something tells me, Hannah, that maybe I know too much," Nancy said. "That's why it happened at our house this time and not at Fenley Place."

She drove home quickly and ran into the house to see the mess, Hannah following behind. The Drews' cozy home had been transformed into a chaotic warehouse of their possessions. And the telephone *was* ringing. It didn't stop even when Nancy lifted the receiver.

She let the phone ring and began investigating immediately. She checked for signs of forced entry into the house or for some evidence left behind.

"Nothing," she said, coming back to the living room. She lifted the ringing phone again and slammed it down in frustration. The phone stopped ringing. But only for a moment. Then it rang again.

"Hello," Nancy said into the receiver.

"Stay away," a muffled voice said. "Stay away from Fenley Place."

"Josh?" Nancy said angrily.

The voice laughed and hung up.

No, it wasn't Josh Petrie's voice. Nancy knew his voice and sarcastic laugh too well. She couldn't place this voice, but she thought she recognized the laugh.

"Someone spoke to you, didn't he?" Hannah asked. "What did he say?"

"He said to stay away from Fenley Place," Nancy said. "And I have the feeling I know what that means. It means that this"—she gestured at the mess in the room—"was just a warning to me. But Fenley Place is still the main target. The Teppingtons are still in danger."

Nancy sat down on a pile of large sofa pillows and wrapped her gold chain necklace around a finger.

"Did you recognize the voice?" Hannah asked.

"I think it was Chris Hitchcock," Nancy said. "But I don't get it. He's a nice guy. I can't believe he'd do this to us or do anything to the Teppingtons."

Hannah Gruen set a lamp back where it belonged, on an end table. "There's usually more to people than what they show us, good and bad," she said.

Nancy thought about what Hannah had just said. Maybe Chris was hiding something. And if he was, *what* was he hiding?

"You're right, Hannah. I should get to know him better, shouldn't I?" Nancy was on her feet, filled with energy. She pushed pieces of furniture back where they belonged. "I should find out what food he likes and what food he hates—or can't eat. And I should find out where he hides his secrets—in a chest of drawers, a suitcase, or a backpack maybe."

"What does all that mean exactly?" Hannah demanded.

"I think it means don't count on me for dinner," Nancy said, jumping over the couch as if it were a high hurdle.

She was in her car and out of the driveway before Hannah could ask her to explain her plan or warn her to be careful.

Nancy drove back to Highland Avenue and mingled with the crew. It didn't take her long to find Jane, Chris Hitchcock's frisbee partner. Nancy simply looked for the tallest head there.

"Do you know where Chris is?" Nancy asked.

Jane got on her walkie-talkie to Chris, but she got no answer. She shrugged her shoulders. "I guess he's not around the set," she told Nancy.

"I've got to find him," Nancy said. "Uh, I found this bottle of his medicine."

"Gee, I didn't know he was sick," Jane said.

"Do you know where he's staying?" Nancy asked.

"Sure," Jane said, nodding her head. "Just about everyone in the crew is staying at the Happy Trails Motel. Is that really the best motel in River Heights?"

"Not exactly," was all Nancy could say about the rundown motel. In fact, the Happy Trails was just about the worst, and definitely the cheapest, motel in River Heights.

"I should have known that's why they stuck us there," Jane said. "Chris's room faces a big neon sign that blinks on and off all night. He calls it the land of the Midnight Sun. He's a funny guy."

"Yes," Nancy said, but she didn't nod her head.

There was just one more thing Nancy needed before going to the Happy Trails Motel—company. If she was going to search Chris Hitchcock's room, she'd need a lookout. Nancy found George in the catering tent and in world's record time she talked her into coming along.

Before they left, George grabbed two leftover sandwiches from a tray, a bag of potato chips, and two cans of soda. They ate their picnic dinner in the car as they drove to the motel.

When they got to the Happy Trails Motel they drove around it first. It was located on a busy road near the heaviest commerical area of River Heights. There were two rooms that faced a large neon sign. The sign belonged to River Heights' only twenty-four-hour health food store, the Healthy Appetite.

"Which one of those two rooms do you think is Chris's?" George asked Nancy. "The one with the lights on, or the one with the lights off?"

"Lights off," Nancy guessed. She pulled into the parking space in front of the dark room.

They walked up to the door. Nancy knocked softly.

"Do not disturb, okay?" a man's gruff voice shouted. "I need my sleep, okay? So get lost, okay?"

The two girls moved quickly down to the next

135

door. Nancy knocked on the door several times, but there was no answer. Evidently, Chris wasn't in his room. She looked at George, who shrugged helplessly. How could they get inside?

Just then, a man in coveralls, carrying a heavy case of tools came around the corner.

"Can I help you?" he asked.

Nancy quickly turned back to the door and gave it a solid kick. "I locked my keys in the room," Nancy told him.

The guy walked straight toward them. "I don't work here. I just fix the TVs," he said. "But who am I to deny two pretty little ladies in distress?" He smiled, then unlocked the door with a pass key and held it open.

"Thanks," Nancy said and closed the door quietly behind her and George. When they heard the man walking away, Nancy reopened the door.

"You wait outside," Nancy said to George, "and knock if I'm in trouble."

Nancy noticed that the room was clean and that Chris kept the place in order. On the dresser there was a photo of Jenny Logan. She had written, "To Chris. Remember me when you get to the top. Jen."

Nancy moved into the bathroom. There, she found fresh towels and soaps in paper wrappers, a can of shaving cream, a razor, and a bottle of after shave lotion that smelled like too-sweet pine needles.

In the medicine cabinet were two different bottles of aspirin tablets, a portable hair dryer, and a tube of toothpaste. There wasn't one bottle with capsules for asthma or allergy.

George knocked on the door, and Nancy's racing pulse almost burst. She ran to open it.

It was George. "Find anything yet?" she asked.

Nancy shook her head.

"Well, try his suitcase, Nancy."

"How do you know I haven't?"

"Because I knew you'd be too polite to look there first," George teased. Then she went outside again to stand guard.

Chris's suitcase was an old, stiff-sided, banged-up black leather bag with the word *CAT* printed near the handle in gold letters.

He probably bought it in a pet store Nancy thought and laughed. Then she stopped laughing because she suddenly realized that *CAT* was not the word *cat*. It was a set of initials—Chris's monogram. *C* for Chris. *A* for, what? But the last initial should be *S* for Smith or *H* for Hitchcock. Not *T*, unless that was a joke, too.

Nancy slowly lifted the lid of the suitcase. Shirts, jeans, and socks packed tight. But in the pouch in the lid, she found something unexpected. It was a color snapshot, twenty years old at least, judging by the hairstyle of the blond young mother in the picture. In her arms was a baby, her new baby. It was a tender picture of mother love. But Nancy's hands trembled as she held it. She recognized the woman!

It was the actress Pamela Teppington.

16

Scene in the Attic

The photograph hypnotized Nancy. The young Pamela Teppington gazed so directly at the camera and smiled so confidently. Her arms were gentle yet protective around the baby.

A knock on the window snapped Nancy out of her thoughts. She slammed down the lid of the suitcase and whirled toward the window.

George was mouthing the words, "Let's go!"

Still holding the photo, Nancy ran to the door. As soon as she opened it, she saw why George was worried. The parking lot was filling up. The movie crew were coming back.

"Chris is probably on his way," George said as they hurried to Nancy's car.

"Good," said Nancy, getting in but not starting the engine. "He's just the person I want to see."

George looked at the photo in Nancy's hand. "Cute picture, but are you sure you should take it?" she asked.

"I don't think it belongs to Chris," was all Nancy said. She turned on her car radio to wait for Chris.

"It's eight twenty-four on the Rick Rondell Oldies Request Show on WRVH," the DJ said. "I'm playing the songs you want to hear. Tonight, Susie wants to hear some Rolling Stones. So I told her to go listen to an avalanche—hahaha! Chuck requested some surfin' oldies, and my mother called and requested that I change my socks more often. Thanks, Mom. Great to know you're listening."

"This guy thinks he's really funny," George said.

"And I just got a call from Jane," said Rick Rondell without taking a breath. "Jane is on the Hank Steinberg movie crew visiting our fair city. She wants to hear *anything* by Elvis Presley. And remember, movie fans, if you're going to the McCauley house to watch the filming, you'd better get there soon."

Suddenly Rick Rondell had Nancy's full attention.

"River Heights police will be closing Highland Avenue in about twenty minutes," Rick went on, "so that the fire trucks can get in and out, if necessary. Hank Steinberg is setting fire to the McCauley house tonight. So bring your own marshmallows!"

Nancy snapped off the radio and started her car.

"What's the hurry, Nancy?"

"Steinberg's changed the shooting schedule," Nancy said. She pulled into traffic quickly and drove with racing driver intensity. "Don't you understand? He's shooting the *fire* scene tonight, not tomorrow. That means it could be getting hot, *too* hot, at Fenley Place right now."

139

The police stopped Nancy at the barricade that blocked off Highland Avenue.

"You can't go through, miss," the officer said.

"I have to. I'm staying at Fenley Place," Nancy explained.

"Fenley Place?" said the officer. "I'd be doing you a favor to keep you away. But go on."

Nancy quickly drove down the street and zipped into the driveway. Across the street, the movie lights were once again shining on the McCauley house, bright as day. The special effects team was setting up gas jets to pump blasts of fire from a window facing the lawn.

A River Heights fire truck was parked nearby just in case the special effects got out of hand. But who would notice if things got out of hand on the other side of the street?

Nancy and George watched for a while from the front lawn of Fenley Place.

"I'm going to run over to Pat Ellis's tent and bring back something to eat," George said. "Want to come?"

"I'd better not," Nancy said. "I'm going to walk around the house."

"I'll be right back," promised George.

Nancy watched George disappear down the block. Then she started her circle around the old house.

Her feet crunched the driveway stones. As she came around to the back of the house, her legs became tangled in a small fallen branch. She almost

140

tripped and fell. It was dark in the backyard and Nancy realized she should have turned on the lights in the house first.

She took a step and something hard under her foot squeaked in pain. Nancy's heart raced and she stepped back quickly. Removing her foot made it squeak again. She reached down toward the sound and her fingers picked up something soft and rubbery.

This is going to be a long night, Nancy Drew, if you let rubber ducks scare you, she thought, picking up the soft rubber toy.

Nancy finished her tour around the house and went inside to wait for George.

Later, the two friends sat around the oversized dining room table, spooning Pat's fudge cake ice cream roll into their mouths. Three long white candles burned in a heavy silver candelabrum that Nancy had placed in the middle of the table. She had decided not to turn on the electric lights in case Fenley Place received a visitor that night—one with arson on his mind. The hot fatty candle wax sputtered.

"You know, all this place needs, to fix it up, is a few gallons of paint and a bulldozer," George said.

"Shh," Nancy said. The candlelight flickered and almost went out. "I think Sara Teppington is right. This house has feelings."

"I wish it had air conditioning," George said, yawning. "I feel like I've been locked in a closet."

They blew out the candles and carried cans of

soda into the living room. Gloom seemed to watch over them. So did the eyes of the carved heads on the mantel.

George flopped down on the couch and yawned again. "Going to work at five-thirty in the morning should be against the law," she said.

Somewhere upstairs the house creaked and stretched as if it were just waking up.

George's head drooped a little more. "I'm not going to fall asleep, Nancy. Honest. But if I just nap for five minutes," she said, "I'll be set for the night."

"No problem," Nancy said.

"Honest. Wake me up. Five minutes, okay?"

George drifted off and for a few moments, Nancy sat in a high-backed chair, listening to voices drifting over from the McCauley house. They were still setting up for the fire scene.

Then, all of a sudden, Nancy knew what to do. She got out of her chair, picked up the photo of Pamela Teppington and the baby, found a flashlight, and climbed the stairs to the attic.

It only took a minute, even in the cramped attic, to find what she was looking for.

Alan Teppington's trunk had been moved back against a wall. She opened the lid.

"Old clothes that don't fit and memories I don't think about" was Alan Teppington's bitter description of the trunk.

If Nancy was right, he, too, was hiding a secret.

She moved some clothing aside until she came to a brown leather photo album. Alan Teppington hadn't mentioned it the first day Nancy was up there.

She opened the book, but a sound startled her. She stood up quickly.

"George?" she asked. Then she said into the silence, "Real juvenile game, George, sneaking around like that."

She knelt down to the photo album again and turned the pages of Alan Teppington's early life. In addition to photos, there were newspaper clippings and stories he had written for his college newspaper. There were high-school pictures of him with a very young woman. It took a moment for Nancy to realize that the woman was Pamela Teppington with dark hair.

She turned the page and saw wedding pictures, showing Pamela as a blond.

Again, she heard a sound. "George, stop playing around," Nancy called into the dark stairway landing. "I want to show you something."

There was no answer. Nancy shook her head. Apparently George wanted to keep playing her little game.

Nancy turned another page. The page was blank, but there were fade marks and an imprint on the self-sticking plastic. A picture had been removed from this page.

She opened the plastic overlay and tried the photo of Pamela and the baby. It fit the outline perfectly.

"George, I was right about the photo," Nancy said.

George's answer wasn't what Nancy had expected. Suddenly she felt a sharp pain on the back of her head. Then there were two photo albums, two Pamela Teppingtons, two of everything—and her head hurt terribly. Nancy stood up for just an instant on wobbly legs, then fell to the floor. The last thing she saw as she blacked out was the yellow and red flames just outside the attic window.

17

Trapped!

George, that hurt. And it wasn't funny. Why aren't you listening? George? George?

A voice was talking in Nancy's dream, a faraway voice. Sometimes Nancy could hear all the words, and sometimes she couldn't. Slowly they became clearer and she realized she was only hearing her own thoughts. When she finally came out of it, she had no idea how long she'd been unconscious.

"George!" Nancy shouted, then winced with pain. Shouting hurt her head. Moving hurt her head, too. She reached up and felt a small lump.

Lying on the floor, looking at the dust, Nancy suddenly remembered the flames outside the window. She struggled to her feet.

"George!" Nancy called to her friend downstairs.

She made it to the window, each step getting easier, surer. Once there, she rested her head against the glass pane and sighed with relief.

There was no fire eating away at the roof of Fenley Place. The flames she'd seen were coming

145

from Bo Aronson's special effects across the street at the McCauley house.

Nancy was beginning to feel stronger. She walked to the attic door. It was closed, although she didn't remember shutting it.

The doorknob rattled and moved in her hand. It did everything a doorknob should do, except open the door.

Try harder, she told herself.

She twisted the knob and pulled as hard as she could, but the door wouldn't open.

"George!" Nancy yelled, pounding on the door. "I'm locked in the attic!"

She kept yelling and pounding on the door with both fists. She tried knocking over boxes and dropping cartons, so George would hear the racket and come upstairs. There was no response. George must not have heard her.

That left the windows. One of them was painted shut. She couldn't budge it. But the other window had to open. It was the one through which the bird had flown.

That window was closed now, too. It wasn't locked—it just refused to open. With a sinking feeling, Nancy realized that someone must have nailed it shut from the outside.

"What's going on?" Nancy asked herself.

Suddenly the footsteps started again. She held her breath. It was the same sound she had heard earlier that afternoon. Rubber track shoes on roof shingles. *He was on the roof.*

She had to get out of the attic, and fast. If she

didn't, she'd soon be trapped inside while the house burned around her!

Nancy lifted a carton and threw it through the window.

I hope someone is watching out there, she thought. She knocked out the remaining shards of glass with her shoe. Then she squeezed out through the window frame.

A lone figure stood on the roof in moonlit silhouette.

"Chris," Nancy called, climbing out onto the roof. *"Chris Teppington."*

The figure froze.

"Don't do it," Nancy pleaded. *"Please."*

"I told you to stay away. I warned you!" Chris called back.

Nancy started to move toward him. There was a click and then the flame of a cigarette lighter glowed under Chris's face.

"Don't come any closer," he said. "Or I'll light the roof."

Nancy looked down and saw a pile of gasoline-soaked newspapers at Chris's feet. She knew he was upset enough to light it. Her only chance was to talk to him, to stall. She hoped someone down on the street, one of the crew members, would hear them and look up.

"I found the photo of Pamela Teppington in your suitcase," Nancy said.

"You stole it, you mean," Chris snapped.

"No, I just put it back where it belonged—in your *father's* scrapbook," Nancy said.

147

"Lucky guess," Chris said.

"No, actually I figured it out," Nancy replied. "When I saw that picture and did a little counting, I realized the baby *had* to be Alan's baby. After that it was easy to figure out that the *T* on your suitcase must stand for Teppington. What's the *A* for?" Nancy asked, although she thought she knew the answer already.

"Alan—just like my father. Is that a joke or what?" Chris said. "Okay, you're real smart. But you can't stop me."

"I was pretty slow about the medicine," Nancy admitted. "It's your asthma medicine isn't it?"

"Yeah," he said. "Allergies run in the family."

Just keep talking, Nancy. Keep *him* talking. Stall. Anything to prevent him from lighting those newspapers. "Why did you tear your name off the label?" Nancy casually sat down on the roof as if she were having a conversation on her front porch.

"Because my doctor in L.A. is a jerk. He writes the prescription in my real name, Chris Teppington," he explained. "I didn't want anyone on the crew to find that out."

"So that's how you knew Alan Teppington was allergic to pineapple," Nancy said. "But I didn't get it, so you called me up. You wanted me to recognize your voice and catch you—admit it."

Suddenly a bright light swept over the roof. Chris covered his eyes. Nancy squinted and looked down to the street.

Just as she had hoped, the movie crew had heard

their voices. And now they were shining the huge klieg lights at the roof of Fenley Place.

"Chris, I don't know what's gone on between you and your dad—" Nancy began, but Chris didn't let her finish the sentence.

"Nothing—nothing's been going on between me and my father. Nothing for twenty years!" he shouted. "He knew my mom was pregnant, but they split up anyway. And he never came, and he never even called. Can you believe that? So now it's my turn to hurt him the way he hurt me."

Nancy looked behind her, away from the bright lights. In the shadows down below she saw someone beginning to climb the oak tree. Unfortunately, Chris saw him too.

"Don't come near me or I'll light it!" Chris warned the onlookers. He lowered the lighter to within inches of the newspapers.

"Chris, it's awful that your dad ignored you. But it doesn't make this right," Nancy said.

Chris laughed at Nancy. "Oh, yeah? What would *you* do?" he shouted. "What would you do if you thought your father was gone, out of your life—and then twenty years later you knocked on a door in a strange town and he's standing there in front of you?"

His words drilled through Nancy's heart. She saw the photos of her mother, who died when Nancy was three, sitting on her dresser at home.

Nancy swallowed hard. "I don't know, Chris. Maybe I'd hug him," she said.

149

"You don't know anything about it," he shouted. "You can't just ask to be loved—not after twenty years."

"I can't think of any other way to do it," Nancy said. "Burning your father's house, scaring two little girls to death—your half-sisters—just doesn't make it."

Chris sighed a long, sad sigh, but then he looked at the cigarette lighter again. "Look down there— they're waiting for a show. Lights, camera, action."

Nancy lunged forward, reaching for Chris. But in the move, she stumbled, fell, and slid on the roof. "Ouch!" she shouted, grabbing her right hand.

"Are you okay?" Chris asked nervously.

Nancy held out her right hand for him to see. It was bleeding profusely.

18

Father and Son

"Oh, no! That was really *stupid* of you!" Chris yelled. He was angry, upset, and worried about Nancy's hand all at once. He put away the lighter and tried to think of what to do.

In that short moment, Spider Hutchings sprang out of the oak tree, overpowered Chris, and forcibly wrested the lighter from his hand.

"There's nothing like having a good stunt man around when you really need one," Nancy said, smiling at Spider.

Spider was sitting on top of Chris now, with his knee pressed into Chris's chest. Chris could hardly breathe.

"Hey, lighten up," Chris said coughing. "Save it for the cameras, okay?"

"What happened to you, kid?" Spider asked. "I don't understand *this* at all."

"That's right, you don't. So butt out," Chris said. He turned his head toward Nancy and asked, "Are you okay?"

Spider looked over for the first time and saw the

blood dripping from Nancy's hand. "That looks nasty," he said to her. "We'd better get you to a doctor quick."

"Oh, it's nothing," Nancy said, bravely. She licked at her wound. "Mmm. In fact, it tastes just like corn syrup with a trace of red dye."

Spider caught on first, and his laughter exploded like a bomb. "I don't believe it!" he shouted. "Fake blood capsules! She fooled us with our own tricks, kid!"

"I broke it in my hand when I knew you were in the tree." Nancy beamed.

Chris didn't seem to think it was as funny as Nancy and Spider did.

In the quiet they heard a siren wailing. Nancy figured that someone across the street must have called the police.

"Well, is everybody ready for a really hot family reunion?" Chris asked.

Spider pulled Chris up, and they climbed back through the attic window and then down the stairs, Nancy following behind. In the living room, Nancy found George still asleep on the couch.

"George, wake up," Nancy said, leaning over her friend.

"Are my five minutes up yet?" asked George drowsily.

"Yes," Nancy said. "And I don't think you should be asleep when the police come."

"Police!" exclaimed George. Then she saw Nancy's bloody hand and gasped.

"It's just a trick, George. A special effect,"

Nancy said reassuringly. She quickly filled George in on the events that had just taken place in the attic and on the roof.

"That's what I get for falling asleep," said George. "I missed all the excitement!"

Just then a police car screeched into the driveway. Chris cracked his knuckles nervously. "Spider," Chris said, "don't you have a wall to jump through or something?"

"You know, a couple of hours ago," Spider said, "you and I were friends. Don't be so sure I haven't changed my mind about you, kid."

Two uniformed police officers knocked at the door, and Nancy let them in. About twenty minutes later, Sergeant Velez arrived, followed by Sara and Alan Teppington. They both looked tired.

"Who was it?" The sergeant threw the question into the room and waited to see who took the bait.

Chris didn't stand up, but he said, "I'm the guy."

Alan Teppington pushed past the sergeant and grabbed a handful of Chris's shirt, jerking him off the ground.

"You little punk!" Alan shouted.

One of the policemen grabbed Alan's arm and held him back, but that didn't turn off his anger.

"Do you know what I'd like to do to you?" Alan shouted, struggling against the uniformed officer.

"What, *Dad?*" Chris asked pointedly.

"What did you say?" Alan shouted.

"I said, 'Hi, Dad.'" Chris meant to spit out the words, but they got caught in his throat on the way out.

"What's going on?" Sara asked Alan with her eyes. But he just shrugged and said, "See? I told you: movie people are nuts!"

Chris laughed shortly. "Well, I guess you can't be expected to recognize me, since you'd already *left* when I was born," he said. "But you knew I existed—that's the part that's so hard to take."

Alan Teppington's mouth opened but he didn't say anything. He just stood there and stared at Chris.

"What's he talking about?" Sergeant Velez asked Alan. Finally, Velez hovered in front of Chris. "What's going on? Who are you, kid?"

"I'm his son," Chris said finally.

Alan Teppington fell backward a step and slumped down onto the couch next to his wife.

"What's this all about?" asked the sergeant in a stern voice.

"See, officer, the truth is," Chris said to Velez in a confidential tone, "he doesn't know for sure. He's got a picture of me in his attic from just after I was born. He's never seen me in the flesh."

Alan Teppington jumped up and pounded on a soft high-backed chair. "How could you do it? You sat in *this* chair," Alan said, "and said to me, 'Hank Steinberg wants this, Hank Steinberg wants that.' You talked to us all afternoon, and you never said a word."

"Hey, Dad, you stayed away for twenty years. *You* never said a word. And I hate you for it." Chris was almost in tears.

Sara was on her feet. Nancy had seen her stand

154

that way many times in school, defending a student or an idea.

"You have no right to talk to someone you don't know like that," Sara said. "Even if he is your father."

"Yes, he does," Alan said. "He does have the right." Then he looked back at his son. "Didn't your mother get married again?"

"Yeah. She must have forgotten to invite you to the wedding," Chris said sarcastically. "She married a rich old movie producer. I think she really likes him; who knows why. I can't stand the man."

Chris snapped his fingers. "That's how he called me when he wanted me to do something for him, which was a lot."

Chris kept snapping his fingers. "After a while, I was convinced he'd forgotten my name. Get the picture? He says that a lot, too. He thinks it's funny."

Chris walked to a chest crowded with photos of Kate and Amy.

"You know," he said, "when Hank asked me to find a spooky old house I thought of River Heights, where my mom had grown up. She was the one who told me about Fenley Place. So I hopped a plane."

He looked around the room, at the walls and arches of Fenley Place. The house seemed to be listening to Chris's story, too.

"The house was perfect," Chris said. "It knocked me out the minute I saw it. Then when I found out that Alan Teppington, *my father*, lived here, I thought I'd introduce myself to you, to my stepmother, and of course to my two half-sisters. But I couldn't do it. You kept yelling about how much you hated movie people. I just sat here hoping the ceiling would fall down or something."

All of a sudden, Chris seemed talked out and tired. He leaned against a chair and looked at his father.

"You know, when your mother and I got divorced," Alan said, "she was making a lot more money than I was. She didn't need me, and she didn't want me around. I was so hurt, I didn't want anything to do with her. It took me years to realize that *you* needed me. But by then I couldn't make the move." He paused and then added, "I'll tell you something: I hate myself for it, too."

"Folks," Sergeant Velez said to the Teppingtons, "it's getting late. Do you want me to take him into custody? Are you going to press charges?"

Sara turned to her husband, but he was looking at Chris.

"No," Alan said. "I won't press charges. But thanks for your help, Sergeant."

"Then good night, Mr. Teppington, Mrs. Teppington," Sergeant Velez said. He and Spider Hutchings walked out together, followed by the uniformed officers. As they were leaving, the sergeant told his people to send the curious crew members back across the street where they belonged.

Sara drove off, as well, to pick up the girls and Boris, who had been dropped at a babysitter's house. And after Nancy and George left, Alan and Chris went for a long walk.

The next day, Nancy, George, and Bess were walking through the River Heights mall.

"So everything was really just movie magic? No ghosts in Fenley Place?" Bess said, with some disappointment.

"Uh-huh," Nancy said. " Chris watched how Bo Aronson blew out the windows, then he stole some small explosives and detonators and used them on Fenley Place."

"The red smoke?" Bess asked.

"Red powder and a remote control detonator," Nancy said.

"The dead dog?"

"Chris kidnapped Boris and then gave the dog a tranquilizer mixed into some food."

"The woman in the window? That was real, I'll bet," said Bess.

"A white nightgown hanging on monofilament wire," Nancy said.

"Hey, Nancy," George said. "Isn't that Deck Burroughs coming out of that shoe store?"

"Quick, Nancy," Bess said. "Spill something on him so he'll talk to us."

But it wasn't necessary. Although he was walking quickly so that he wouldn't be noticed by too many people, Deck Burroughs stopped when he saw Nancy and her friends.

He shook hands with George and Bess, and said,

"Nice meeting you, again," as he shook hands with Nancy.

Then he was gone in a crowd of admirers.

Nancy, Bess, and George walked on. They bought new swim suits in The Cool Pool and even ran into Chris Teppington coming out of Shirts Till It Hurts.

"I can't believe I ran into you guys," he said. "Perfect timing. I have a present for each of you." He held up a large paper bag.

"How's it going?" George asked.

"You mean with my dad?" Chris said. "It's a little strange, getting to know him and all. He's been quiet but that's okay. He's turning out to be an all-right guy. And I like Kate and Amy and Sara. They want me to stay awhile after Hank leaves, but I don't know. Maybe I will."

"I'm glad," Nancy said.

"Anyway," Chris said, "I got you guys something. It's my way of saying thanks." He took three *Terror Weekend* T-shirts out of the paper bag.

"Oh no! Are they selling those at the shirt store?" Bess said. "I wanted to be the only one in River Heights with a *Terror Weekend* T-shirt."

"Don't worry," Chris said, smiling. "These are exclusives. I just took them to the store to have them, uh, monogrammed."

As he unfolded the shirts, the girls could see that the back of each one was printed with the question that had pursued them all through this case— Screamer, Bleeder, or Corpse?